Ashleigh doesn't want to ride anymore.

"Do you want to go for a ride tomorrow after school, Ash?" Mona asked. "We could ride over to the Wortons' and see what's happening with the race camp."

Ashleigh shook her head and bumped Stardust into a canter without looking back at her friend. She knew if she turned around, she'd see the same worried look on Mona's face that her parents had worn just an hour before. Why couldn't they all stop worrying about her? She was fine. Dreamer was the one they needed to worry about. It was her life that would never be the same again.

She cantered the rest of the way to Edgardale without glancing back at her best friend or toward the Wortons' farm and their race camp. She wasn't interested in going to the camp anymore; she wasn't interested in riding at all.

Collect all the books in the Thoroughbred series

#1 *A Horse Called Wonder*
#2 *Wonder's Promise*
#3 *Wonder's First Race*
#4 *Wonder's Victory*
#5 *Ashleigh's Dream*
#6 *Wonder's Yearling*
#7 *Samantha's Pride*
#8 *Sierra's Steeplechase*
#9 *Pride's Challenge*
#10 *Pride's Last Race*
#11 *Wonder's Sister*
#12 *Shining's Orphan*
#13 *Cindy's Runaway Colt*
#14 *Cindy's Glory*
#15 *Glory's Triumph*
#16 *Glory in Danger*
#17 *Ashleigh's Farewell*
#18 *Glory's Rival*
#19 *Cindy's Heartbreak*
#20 *Champion's Spirit*
#21 *Wonder's Champion*
#22 *Arabian Challenge*
#23 *Cindy's Honor*
#24 *The Horse of Her Dreams*
#25 *Melanie's Treasure*
#26 *Sterling's Second Chance*
#27 *Christina's Courage*
#28 *Camp Saddlebrook*
#29 *Melanie's Last Ride*
#30 *Dylan's Choice*
#31 *A Home for Melanie*
#32 *Cassidy's Secret*
#33 *Racing Parker*
#34 *On the Track*
#35 *Dead Heat*
#36 *Without Wonder*
#37 *Star in Danger*
#38 *Down to the Wire*
#39 *Living Legend*
#40 *Ultimate Risk*
#41 *Close Call*
#42 *The Bad-Luck Filly*
#43 *Fallen Star*
#44 *Perfect Image*
#45 *Star's Chance*
#46 *Racing Image*
#47 *Cindy's Desert Adventure*
#48 *Cindy's Bold Start*
#49 *Rising Star*
#50 *Team Player*
#51 *Distance Runner**

Collect all the books in the Ashleigh series

#1 *Lightning's Last Hope*
#2 *A Horse for Christmas*
#3 *Waiting for Stardust*
#4 *Good-bye, Midnight Wanderer*
#5 *The Forbidden Stallion*
#6 *A Dangerous Ride*
#7 *Derby Day*
#8 *The Lost Foal*
#9 *Holiday Homecoming*
#10 *Derby Dreams*
#11 *Ashleigh's Promise*
#12 *Winter Race Camp*

THOROUGHBRED Super Editions
Ashleigh's Christmas Miracle
Ashleigh's Diary
Ashleigh's Hope
Samantha's Journey

ASHLEIGH'S Thoroughbred Collection
Star of Shadowbrook Farm
The Forgotten Filly
Battlecry Forever!

* coming soon

THOROUGHBRED

WINTER RACE CAMP

CREATED BY
JOANNA CAMPBELL

WRITTEN BY
CHRIS PLATT

HarperEntertainment
An Imprint of HarperCollins*Publishers*

HarperEntertainment
An Imprint of HarperCollins*Publishers*
10 East 53rd Street, New York, NY 10022–5299

Produced by 17th Street Productions, Inc., an Alloy Online, Inc., company

HarperCollins books are available at special quantity discounts for bulk purchases for sales promotions, premiums, or fund-raising.
For information please call or write:
Special Markets Department, HarperCollins Publishers Inc.,
10 East 53rd Street, New York, NY 10022-5299.
Telephone: (212) 207-7528. Fax: (212) 207-7222.

ISBN 0-06-106826-8

First printing: January 2002

Printed in the United States of America

Visit HarperEntertainment on the World Wide Web at
www.harpercollins.com

❖ 10 9 8 7 6 5 4 3 2 1

To my nephews, Jason and Justin Duby

"Ashleigh, Smashleigh," the boy called, his singsong voice ringing out across the school hallway. "You'd better run home and study so you won't do so badly on your math test next time. And don't forget to brush the hay out of your hair before you come back to school!"

Eleven-year-old Ashleigh Griffen cringed as she hurriedly gathered her books and shoved them into her book bag. She turned to her best friend, Mona Gardner, and grimaced. "Let's get out of here."

Mona's short dark hair bobbed as she nodded vigorously and followed her friend out the school door and down the steps. "That Vince Tully is such a pain," Mona said in exasperation. "Why doesn't he pick on somebody else?"

Ashleigh glanced nervously over her shoulder. "I'm an easy target," she said. "I'm little. He never picks on anybody his own size."

"Hmpf!" Mona scoffed. "There *is* no one his own size. Vince is the biggest kid in school."

"What's the matter, Smashleigh?" Vince's voice trailed after them. "You've got to hurry home to your horses? Don't forget to change your shoes next time. I can smell the manure on them from three classrooms away!" The bully let out a hearty laugh through the open school doors.

Ashleigh glanced over her shoulder at the tall, thin kid with dark hair and hard eyes. "Leave us alone!" she muttered as she climbed onto the school bus and settled into the seat behind the driver, just in case Vince decided to follow them onto the bus. He only lived a mile away from her, but luckily for her, he rode another bus. She glanced out the window, relieved to see that he had given up his mean-spirited game. "I just hope he doesn't ever show up at Edgardale," she whispered to Mona.

"He wouldn't dare!" Mona exclaimed. "Your father would send him packing."

Ashleigh brushed a strand of her long dark hair out of her eyes and tucked her winter gloves into her coat pockets. "The teachers all think Vince is great because he gets good grades. They don't believe how horrible he is. But one of these days his pranks are going to catch up to him," she predicted.

"Look, there's Jamie and Lynne." Mona pointed to

their horse pals as the girls walked past, heading for their own bus.

Ashleigh smiled and waved. "Jamie thinks I should report Vince to the principal, but I'm afraid that will only make him worse."

Mona tucked her backpack under the seat in front of her. "Maybe she's right," she said. "Maybe you should, Ash."

Ashleigh leaned back against the seat and stared out the bus window as they pulled away from the school. All she wanted to do just then was go home and be with her horses. Her chestnut mare, Stardust, all the broodmares, and her little brother Rory's molasses-colored pony, Moe, would be happy to see her, as always. And now there was a new horse in the barn.

Trainer Mike Smith, who was a good friend of the family, had brought a new three-year-old filly to train at Edgardale. With the breeding farm's peace and quiet and the Wortons' training track next door, Mike felt the flighty filly would train better at Edgardale than she would at the racetrack.

The bus topped the rise, and Ashleigh smiled as Edgardale came into view. It was a small farm compared to some of the large Thoroughbred breeding and training establishments in the area, but to Ashleigh it was perfect.

The large brown broodmare barn and white two-story farmhouse stood amidst acres of rolling white-fenced paddocks and pastures. It was the last week in January, and the fields were brown. The large oak, maple, and Bradford pear trees stood with their bare branches stretching skyward. But Ashleigh knew that in a couple more months they'd have new foals standing beside their mothers, knee deep in the rich Kentucky bluegrass.

"Here we are." Ashleigh reached for her bag as the bus rolled to a stop halfway between Edgardale and the Gardners' farm.

Mona followed Ashleigh off the bus. "Don't forget I'm catching a ride to the feed store with you and your parents tonight."

"Okay, I'll see you in a couple of hours." Ashleigh waved as they parted, then slung her book bag over her shoulder and jogged down Edgardale's long gravel driveway. Her parents and Jonas McIntire, Edgardale's only hired hand, were just bringing the yearlings in when she arrived at the barn.

Mrs. Griffen tucked her blond hair beneath her red stocking cap and waved Ashleigh toward the house. "Hurry and change your clothes, Ash. Mike and Mr. Rosen will be here soon. Mike is expecting you to help with Dreamer."

Mr. Griffen poked his head out the barn door and nodded. "And be ready for an ambush from your little brother." He chuckled. "Moe bucked Rory off today, and he's looking for some words of encouragement."

Ashleigh smiled to herself as she ran to the house. Moe had bucked her off plenty of times, too. The cantankerous Shetland-Welsh cross had belonged to Ashleigh until she outgrew the little gelding and passed him on to her five-year-old brother.

She opened the door to the house and kicked off her shoes in the hallway entrance.

"Hi, Ash!" a small voice called from the living room.

Ashleigh smiled as Rory's red-gold hair popped up from the couch, where he sat watching a rerun of an old horse movie. "I heard you had a rough day with Moe," Ashleigh said.

Rory nodded solemnly, and Ashleigh smiled.

"I'll help you work with him this weekend, okay?" she promised.

Rory smiled brightly. "You're my favorite sister, Ash." Then he turned his attention back to the television.

"Yeah, right," Ashleigh called with a laugh as she turned to run up the stairs. "That'll only last until Caroline bakes you a batch of chocolate chip cookies."

She opened the door to her bedroom and wrinkled

her nose. The air reeked of perfume. She crossed the room and threw the window wide open, not caring that it was winter and freezing cold outside. "Yuck!" she muttered in disgust as she surveyed the teen magazines and nail polish that littered her sister's side of the room.

At thirteen, Caroline had discovered telephone gossip, makeup, and movie stars. She was the only member of the Griffen family who wasn't passionate about horses.

Ashleigh ignored her sister's mess and quickly changed into jeans and a heavy sweatshirt, then headed back down the stairs. She yanked on her boots in the hallway and scooted out the door. Mike was just coming up the driveway when she reached the barnyard.

"Better get Dreamer groomed," the stocky trainer hollered out the truck window as he pulled to a stop in front of the barn. "Mr. Rosen will be here in a few minutes, and he wants to check his filly over. We're going to take Dreamer to Turfway Park tomorrow for an official work."

Ashleigh grabbed Dreamer's halter and headed for the filly's stall. She was always happy to see Mike, but Jonathan Rosen was like a burr under a saddle blanket. He always managed to rub people the wrong way. She picked up the bucket of brushes, knowing that the wealthy Thoroughbred owner would notice every patch of dirt she missed.

Stardust thrust her head over the top of the door and nickered when she heard Ashleigh's voice.

"Hey, girl, I bet you'd like to go for a ride, wouldn't you?" Ashleigh asked as she ran a hand down Stardust's white blaze. "Sorry, but you're going to have to wait until we get back from Dreamer's work at the track tomorrow." She slipped the mare a carrot and smiled as the chestnut noisily munched the treat.

Mrs. Griffen handed Ashleigh a small fuzzy towel. "Rub Dreamer with this when you're done brushing her," she suggested. "It'll help bring out the shine in her coat."

Ashleigh smiled her thanks. Her mother and father both knew how meticulous Mr. Rosen was. They were always a little on edge when the owner visited Edgardale. Ashleigh hated to see her parents catering to his whims, but they couldn't afford not to. He might wish to purchase one of their yearlings someday. Ashleigh cringed at the thought. She wanted *all* of Edgardale's sale horses to go to loving homes with owners who cared about more than just the money or prestige a winning horse could bring.

Dream Time stretched her elegant head over the top of the stall door and nickered to Ashleigh, nibbling on her coat as the girl tried to slip the halter over her head.

"You behave yourself," Ashleigh warned playfully as she led the rose-gray filly from the stall and hooked her into the crossties. Dreamer shoved her with her muzzle, and Ashleigh giggled as she removed the hidden carrot the filly was looking for. "You've got a nose like a bloodhound, and you look like one, too," she teased. But as she stood back to admire the leggy racer, she knew that statement was far from the truth. Dreamer was gorgeous!

At only three years old, Dream Time already stood sixteen hands. That was five feet four inches at the withers. She had long, delicate legs, a deep chest, and powerful hindquarters for driving down the homestretch to the finish line. She was sired by one of the top stallions in the country, and out of a mare that had produced multiple stakes winners. The filly was definitely born to run. Ashleigh was thrilled that Mike had talked Mr. Rosen into bringing her to Edgardale to train.

She picked up the rubber currycomb and began rubbing it in circles across the filly's dappled coat to loosen any dirt, following it with swift flicks of the stiff bristled brush before going over the gray's entire body with a soft finishing brush. She laughed at the way the filly's lips wriggled when she hit a particularly ticklish spot.

She was just going over Dreamer's shining coat with a soft rag when her father poked his head into the barn and warned her that Dreamer's owner had arrived. Quickly Ashleigh snapped a lead rope onto the filly's leather halter and unhooked her from the crossties. Mike and Mr. Rosen were standing by the front paddock when she led the gray from the barn.

"Bring Dreamer into the paddock and walk her a bit so Mr. Rosen can see her," Mike told her.

Dreamer bowed her neck and pranced, swinging her hindquarters toward the two men as Ashleigh walked her through the gate.

"Looks like she's full of pep this afternoon," Mike said with a chuckle.

"Are you sure that little girl should be handling my filly?" the tall, pudgy owner asked. He squinted at Ashleigh and ran a nervous hand over his balding head.

Mike clapped the man on the back and nodded toward Ashleigh as she led the flighty gray around in a large circle. "If it weren't for Ashleigh, Dreamer would really be a handful," he said. "Ashleigh knows what she's doing, and Dreamer stays a lot calmer with her around."

Mr. Rosen turned up his nose and huffed. "Well, it's fine for the girl to handle her here at Edgardale, where we're out of the public's eye, but when we get onto the racetrack, we'll want to get a real groom for the filly. We want to present the right image, you know. Image is everything."

Ashleigh pursed her lips and glared at Mr. Rosen. He didn't deserve to own a horse like Dreamer. He was far more interested in the attention his finely bred horses brought him than the horses themselves.

"Give her a couple more laps, and then put her back in her stall," Mike said as he led Mr. Rosen toward the barn's office.

Ashleigh circled the filly for several more minutes, then led her to the gate and fumbled with the latch. Dreamer danced on the end of the rope and bumped her nose into Ashleigh's shoulder.

"Knock it off," Ashleigh warned, giving a tug on the lead rope.

Startled, Dreamer rose on her hind legs and pawed the air with her hooves, barely missing Ashleigh. Then her feet touched the ground and she shook her head, sending her long black mane into a disarray of tangles.

Ashleigh stumbled backward, colliding with the wooden fence post. She was frightened, but if she didn't get control of the situation, the filly might take to the air again, and this time she might not be so lucky. "Dreamer, whoa!" Ashleigh cried, and pulled down hard on the lead rope once more.

Dreamer pricked her little fox ears and snorted, but she quit her misbehaving and thrust her muzzle into Ashleigh's cheek, whuffing great clouds of breath into the chilly air.

Ashleigh quickly looked around to see if anyone had witnessed the scene. Fortunately, everyone was in the barn. If Mr. Rosen had seen the filly act up, Ashleigh knew, she wouldn't have been allowed to continue working with the flighty Thoroughbred.

Her hands were trembling as she led the gray back to the barn. She wouldn't tell anyone except Mona about this incident—and she hoped it wouldn't happen again. She led the filly into her stall and took off her halter. "What got into you today?" Ashleigh asked. Dreamer nuzzled her shoulder, and she lifted her hand to stroke the filly's soft nose.

Mike stopped by the stall. "Everything okay?"

Ashleigh managed a quick nod. She didn't dare speak, fearing that her voice might give her away.

"I'll be here to pick you up before the rooster crows tomorrow morning," Mike said. "Mr. Rosen wants Dreamer worked before too many people get to the racetrack. He's hoping he can keep this filly's speed a secret and cash in a good bet on her first race."

Mr. Griffen brought a full hay net into the stall and tied it on the hook in the corner. He stood back to admire Dreamer. "She's the kind of horse I'd love to have in my broodmare barn," he said.

Mike chuckled. "You could always make Mr. Rosen an offer. He hasn't left yet."

Derek Griffen pulled off his hat and dusted the brim, then set it firmly on his head. "The breeding fee on this filly's sire was fifty thousand dollars," he said. "And that doesn't include the money it cost to raise her, or your training fees, Mike. I'm afraid Edgardale couldn't afford to buy her, even if she were for sale, but it's nice to dream."

Ashleigh was quick to agree. "She'd make a great cross on the stallion we've got picked out for Go Gen and Althea this year."

Mr. Griffen nodded. "Well, let's not waste any more time fantasizing. It's time to get back to work. Ash, you'd better get started on your stalls. I'll be leaving for the feed store in about an hour. We'll pick up Mona on the way."

Ashleigh glanced at her watch. She'd barely have enough time to take care of Stardust and finish her stalls, but if she hurried, she'd make it. She didn't want to miss going to the feed store, which also had a tack shop. They had so much great stuff there. With her birthday only a few months away, she could get started on her wish list.

She put her mare away, reached for the pitchfork and wheelbarrow, and set to work cleaning her share of the stalls. She had barely finished dumping her last wheelbarrow load when she heard her father calling for her. She put away the cleaning tools and ran for the old feed truck.

Mona was waiting for them at the end of her driveway. Ashleigh scooted over to make room for her. "Ready to visit your saddle?" she asked her friend.

Mona grinned as she buckled her seat belt. "I've got three hundred dollars saved so far. My parents said they'd pay for half the saddle if I could raise the rest of the money myself," she explained. "I'm going to be cleaning stalls on weekends at the barn where I take my jumping lessons. I should have the money saved by the first show of the season."

They pulled into the store parking lot. The girls scrambled out of the car as soon as the engine was turned off.

Ashleigh followed Mona into the store. They went straight to the tack section.

"Here it is." Mona pointed to the dark brown English saddle on display.

"It's beautiful!" Ashleigh said. She'd had her eye on that saddle, too, but when she'd asked her parents about buying it, they had told her that Edgardale's bank account was far too low. She'd have to make do with her old saddle for at least another year.

She looked at the display of new bridles that hung on the wall. Maybe she'd be able to talk her parents into one of those for a birthday gift.

"Ash, look!" Mona said, pointing to a flyer posted on the wall of the tack section. "The Wortons are having a race camp for kids at their farm! It says it's going to be after school on Wednesdays, and on weekends." She pulled one of the extra flyers off the wall and handed it to Ashleigh.

Ashleigh felt her fingers shake with excitement as she read the piece of paper. "They're going to bring in top jockeys and trainers to give talks on racing!" She met Mona's eyes and smiled broadly. "The Wortons' farm is right next door to Edgardale. My parents *have* to let me go!"

"Oh, no!" Mona pointed to the bottom of the flyer. "Look at the price."

Ashleigh felt her stomach flop. There was no way she could come up with the amount of money it cost to go to the camp. She crumpled the piece of paper and crammed it into the pocket of her jeans. "I guess that's the end of that," she said dejectedly. She took a deep breath and blew through her bangs.

"Maybe your parents will help you pay for it," Mona suggested. "This camp is perfect for you, Ash. You've always wanted to be a jockey. Your parents have got to let you go!"

Ashleigh felt her hopes begin to rise. "It *is* a lot of money, but maybe Mom and Dad will think it's worth the cost." She glanced at Mona, and a thought came to her. "Hey, do you want to go to the camp, too? It says that the campers will work together with a partner. Each pair of campers works with a racehorse and prepares it for its first race. We could be partners!"

Mona ran her hand lovingly over the new saddle. "It would be fun, Ash, but I'm more into jumping than racing. I've got to put my money toward this new saddle so Frisky and I can do better in our jumping classes this show season."

Ashleigh nodded in understanding. It would be great to have her best friend at camp with her, but she was sure she'd get another good partner at the camp, someone who was just as excited about racing Thoroughbreds as she was.

Mr. Griffen called from the front of the store. "Ash, I'm pulling around to load the feed. Be ready to leave in ten minutes."

"Okay, Dad," she called in return.

"Are you going to ask your parents about the camp when you get home?" Mona asked.

Ashleigh shrugged. "I think it'll be better if I wait

until dinner. Everyone is more relaxed then." She ran her hands over a pair of reins made of nice, soft leather and frowned. Who was she kidding? There would never be a good time to ask her parents to send her to an expensive horse camp. She might as well ask right away. The answer wouldn't be any different later on that night.

They finished looking at the tack and then went to the back of the store, where her father was helping the feed man load grain into the old pickup's bed.

Mr. Griffen looked up and smiled. "Did you find something you like?" he asked.

Ashleigh nodded and handed him the flyer. "The Wortons are having a race camp for kids. They're going to bring in top jockeys and trainers to work with the campers."

Mr. Griffen glanced at the flyer and hefted a bag of rolled oats onto the truck. He turned and cocked a curious brow in Ashleigh's direction. "I suppose you want to go?"

"You bet!" Ashleigh said, beginning to feel a little more at ease. "It starts in three weeks. They're going to hold the camp on Wednesday nights after school and on weekends. I could learn a lot, Dad. I really want to go."

Mr. Griffen waited for the feed man to toss in the

last bag of oats, then he closed the tailgate. "I don't think there will be a problem with you going, Ash. Your grades are okay, and you've kept up with your chores. How much does it cost?" He glanced at the flyer again and frowned.

Ashleigh took a deep breath and then spoke quickly to get all the words out. "It's expensive, but it will be worth it, Dad. I could learn so much, and I'll pay you back every penny of it. I promise."

"Ashleigh," Mr. Griffen said softly as he lifted her chin with one finger and gave her a sympathetic smile, "I know how much the camp would mean to you, but it's way out of our budget." He opened the truck door and motioned for her and Mona to climb in. "You know this time of year is always difficult at Edgardale because we're putting out all the money for breeding fees on the mares. I'm really sorry, honey. Your mother and I would love to send you to that camp, but it's just not feasible now. Maybe Mike can introduce you to some jockeys at the track." He started the truck and pulled out of the feed store parking lot.

Ashleigh tipped her head back, staring at the roof of the old truck. She felt the hot prick of tears sting her eyes and spill onto her cheeks, and she swiped at them angrily with the back of her hand. She had known her parents' answer would be no, but now it was so final.

Mona leaned over, and Ashleigh heard her friend whisper, "I'm sorry."

She stifled a sob. Twenty lucky kids would get to go to the Wortons' race camp, but she'd be stuck looking over the fence at them. It wasn't fair!

Ashleigh rose before the sun came up the next morning. She ate a quick bowl of cereal and went to the barn to prepare for the trip to Turfway Park. Mr. Rosen wanted Dreamer worked while there were very few people around, so they'd need to get to the racetrack by 6 A.M. to be sure she'd be one of the first horses clocked.

She heard the sound of Mike's truck and trailer pulling into the drive just as she was putting on the last shipping boot. She snapped the lead rope on Dreamer's halter and led her from the barn, waiting while Mike parked the truck and opened the horse trailer door. After a few head tosses and snorts, the filly walked into the trailer without a fight.

Ashleigh settled into the pickup and fastened her seat belt. Her mother and father were just leaving the house to do their morning chores as the truck and trailer rolled out of the stable area. She waved to her parents, then closed her eyes and leaned back into the seat cushion, hoping to catch a quick nap along the way. She hadn't slept very well the night before, with the race camp weighing heavily on her mind.

Even now she couldn't sleep. Her mind worked as the miles passed by, thinking about the Wortons' race camp. There had to be some way she could go. She had a few hundred dollars in her savings account from odd jobs she had done for neighboring farms and around the track. Maybe the Wortons would lower the fee for her since she was their neighbor, and let her do some extra work at their farm to help pay her tuition. *That might work!* she thought excitedly. When she got home from the track, she would ride Stardust over and talk to her neighbors.

She opened her eyes and sat a little taller in her seat. It wasn't long before they exited I-75 onto Turfway Road and the gray and beige concrete barns of the stables came into view.

Mike pulled onto the race grounds and showed his trainer's license to the guard at the gate. The man waved them through, and Ashleigh felt her excitement begin to rise as she viewed the long-legged Thoroughbreds through the early morning light. Grooms were just beginning to start their morning chores, and several horses had already been placed on the hotwalkers so their stalls could be cleaned.

They pulled up to the receiving barns, and Ashleigh recognized Mr. Rosen waiting by an open stall.

"Time's a-wasting," he hollered as they stepped from the truck.

Dreamer backed out quickly when the door was opened and stood with her head held high, her nostrils flared to catch all the new smells. Her muscles quivered and her ears pricked toward the racetrack in anticipation of the coming run.

"Let's get moving!" Mr. Rosen ordered. "I want that filly on the track in ten minutes. I'll go tell the clocker we're here."

Ashleigh groaned silently. Mr. Rosen was the type of owner that trainers despised. He had hired Mike to train his horse, but he constantly interfered with Mike's training routine, and when the short, stocky trainer tried to hold his ground, Mr. Rosen reminded him that *he* was paying Mike's salary, and if he didn't get what he wanted, he'd take his horse elsewhere.

Ashleigh flashed Mike an understanding smile and gathered Dreamer's tack while he led the filly to her stall. They quickly put the saddle in place and slipped the bridle over her ears.

"I'd like to run up to the race office and grab a condition book for the first week's races, but I'm afraid Mr. Rosen will send out a search party for us if we're not on the track in the next two minutes," Mike joked. "I guess I can pick it up on the way out."

The gallop boy arrived, and Mike led Dreamer from the stall. Ashleigh held the gray's head while the trainer legged the boy up and gave him his instructions, then she led the horse and rider out to the racetrack. When they reached the entrance gate, she unhooked the snap from the filly's bit and took her place on the rail beside Mike.

Several horses galloped past, and Ashleigh watched the way the riders handled them. She wondered if any of these jockeys would be at the race camp.

Ashleigh glanced down the track's outside rail to where Mr. Rosen stood a few feet away. The tall, balding man held binoculars in his hand and had a worried look on his face.

"That gallop boy looks mighty puny," Mr. Rosen said as he adjusted the binoculars for a closer look. "Are you sure he can hold Dreamer back for a slow work?" he asked Mike. "I don't want anybody to know what kind of speed this filly has. If she runs away with the boy, the public will find out how fast Dreamer is, and I won't be able to cash in on race day."

"He'll do just fine," Mike assured the owner.

A large chestnut horse sped past, and Ashleigh felt her mouth drop open. "Oh, my gosh, that's him!" She pointed to the wiry jockey in the irons. "That's Jack Dale. The number one rider on the East Coast!"

Mr. Rosen put down his binoculars and smiled. "I had a talk with Jack's agent this morning. Jack's going to ride Dreamer in her first race."

"Really?" Ashleigh's heart jumped at the thought. If Dreamer won her first race with Jack aboard, Ashleigh might be able to join them in the win photo, and she'd have a picture to treasure forever!

"Of course," Mr. Rosen scoffed. "I only use the best riders for my horses. That way I know I'll be in the money."

Ashleigh frowned. It seemed as though all Mr. Rosen ever cared about was money.

"Here she comes." Mike pointed to Dreamer as she rounded the turn at a gallop, heading for the half-mile starting pole.

"Is she going too fast?" Mr. Rosen leaned on the rail with his stopwatch, ready to time the filly. He clicked the button when she reached the red-and-white-striped half-mile pole.

Mike winked at Ashleigh as he tried to calm the owner's nerves. "She's going great, Mr. Rosen." He slapped the man good-naturedly on the back. "You'll get the slow work you want, and you'll cash in on your big bet on race day."

Ashleigh glanced at the second hand on her watch, noting that Dreamer had run the first quarter mile in twenty-seven seconds. Twelve seconds per furlong was considered a good solid pace for an eighth of a mile. Dreamer's time for the quarter was right where they wanted it—fast enough to qualify as an official work, but plenty slow enough that word wouldn't get out that they had a potential stakes horse on their hands.

Ashleigh shaded her eyes as she stared across the track to where Dreamer was set to run down the stretch to the finish line. She could see that the gallop boy had a tight hold on the gray, and Dreamer was fighting him.

When another horse galloped up behind the filly, Dreamer tossed her head and grabbed the bit in her teeth, sprinting forward with a burst of speed.

Ashleigh sucked in her breath and stood on her toes, making seesawing motions with her hands, as if she were the rider on the horse's back, trying to slow the filly down. It took the kid almost a furlong to get Dreamer back under control.

"I knew it!" Mr. Rosen screamed as he thumped his

hand against the railing. "That boy was too weak to hold my filly. Now Dreamer's run too fast a time!"

Mike rolled his eyes at Mr. Rosen's outburst. He looked at his stopwatch. "It's not that bad, Jonathan," he said in a calming tone. "She worked the half mile in forty-eight seconds. That's a good work, but it won't be the best time turned in today."

Mr. Rosen rubbed his brow and held up his stopwatch. "But she ran the last quarter mile in twenty-two seconds with the boy practically standing in the irons!" he sputtered, then stomped over to the gap to wait for the horse and rider to return.

"I hope you realize what you've done, young man!" Mr. Rosen chastised as the kid rode Dreamer off the track.

The gallop boy looked surprised by the attack. "I—I'm sorry," he stammered as he worked the knot from his reins and kicked his feet from the irons. "She only got away from me for a moment. I got her slowed back down within a furlong."

"She shouldn't have gotten away at all!" Mr. Rosen snapped.

Mike interrupted the owner's tirade. "That's enough, Jonathan. I'll handle it from here." He waited for the rider to dismount. "You did a fine job, son," he said quietly, and handed the boy his gallop wage. Then

Ashleigh followed as he led Dreamer back to the receiving barn.

Mr. Rosen was waiting for them at the barn. His face was mottled with red blotches. "I'm telling you, Mike, that work will wreck our odds. I probably won't be able to get more than ten to one on her now."

Mike handed Dreamer off to Ashleigh and motioned for her to lead the filly to the wash rack. "One of the track grooms will help you bathe Dreamer," he said. "I'm going to have a private word with Mr. Rosen before he leaves." He winked and handed her the wash bucket and scraper. "I'll be back to put Dreamer on the hotwalker when you're finished."

"I can walk her by hand," Ashleigh volunteered.

Mike glanced at the filly as she danced on the end of the lead rope Ashleigh held. "She's still pretty squirrelly. There's a lot more commotion here than there is at Edgardale," the trainer said. "I don't want to take the chance of Dreamer pulling any shenanigans and getting away. I'm afraid that would send poor Mr. Rosen over the edge." He chuckled as he turned to go meet the demanding owner.

Ashleigh took her time bathing the gray filly. She enjoyed being part of the action at the track. She looked around wistfully at the other grooms who were cleaning stalls, hanging hay nets, or preparing racers for their morning gallops. That was exactly the kind of thing they'd do at the race camp.

Mike returned just as she finished with Dreamer's bath, and placed the filly on the four-armed automatic hotwalker. There were two other horses on the machine. They stopped and looked on curiously as Ashleigh shut off the walker so Dreamer could be snapped onto the rope that hung from the walker arm. When she turned the power back on, all three horses bucked and played for a few seconds before settling down and walking in the circle of wood chips.

Dreamer tossed her head and jigged sideways when she heard the clang of the starting gate in the distance. Then she settled down, walking steadily around the circle with the other horses.

Mike hooked his thumb toward the office buildings. "I'm going to stop by the race office to pick up a condition book. Keep an eye on Dreamer. I'll be right back."

Ashleigh sat on a bale of hay and watched the gray filly circle the walker. Dreamer tossed her head and stamped her feet, seeming to get more and more agitated with each new sound she heard in the active barn area. "Easy, girl," she called to the flighty filly. Now she knew why Mike wanted Dreamer to train at Edgardale. The racetrack was too much of a distraction for her.

One of the grooms turned off the walker to water his horse. Ashleigh picked up her water bucket and approached Dreamer, but the starting gate clanged open once more, and the startled filly snorted and reared high into the air, pawing with her front legs and pulling against the lines that held her.

"Whoa!" Ashleigh cried as she stepped back out of harm's way, but the filly only touched down briefly before she reared again. This time there was the awful sound of metal on metal as Dreamer pawed at the walker arm, which stood eight feet off the ground.

Ashleigh felt her stomach knot and her heart stop as Dreamer's front legs hooked over the walker arm. The filly squealed in fright when she realized she was stuck, and several grooms and trainers, including Mike, came running.

Ashleigh moved forward to help rescue Dreamer, but one of the men stopped her. "It's too dangerous," the tall man cautioned. "You wait here while we get her down." He turned to several of the grooms. "Turn off the power and get those other two horses off there. We're going to have to tip the walker so she can slide her legs off and free herself."

Ashleigh held her breath as the men worked quickly to free the filly. Fortunately, Dreamer seemed to realize she was in big trouble and ceased her struggles, but

Ashleigh could hear the filly's ragged breathing and see the whites of her eyes as they rolled in fear. Somebody pulled the quick-release snap on Dreamer's halter just before they tipped the big piece of machinery on its side. The filly slid free of the walker, and Mike lunged for her halter.

"Get the vet!" Mike hollered, snapping the lead rope onto Dreamer's halter and checking her front legs. He shook his head and quickly led the filly into her stall.

"Is she all right?" Ashleigh ran to catch up with the trainer.

Mike shook his head. "I don't know. She seems to be walking okay, but those tendons took a beating on that metal arm."

"It's all my fault!" Ashleigh cried. "I should have stopped her." The tears ran unchecked down her face, and she brushed them away with her sleeve as she tried to choke back a sob.

Mike laid a reassuring hand on Ashleigh's shoulder. "There's nothing you could have done to stop her," he said. "If you'd tried, you might have been badly hurt."

"But there must have been something I could have done to stop her from rearing!"

Mike handed her his handkerchief. "Ashleigh, this could have happened whether you were here or not. It's not your fault."

The vet arrived, and Ashleigh stood back to let him enter the stall. The man went over every inch of the gray and took several X rays. When he was done he dusted his hands on his coveralls and stepped from the stall.

"I'll have these developed immediately," he said, placing the X rays on the seat of his truck. "I should have the results by the time you get back to Edgardale, but I'd say you probably don't have anything to worry about. You guys were very fortunate," the vet added with a smile. "The filly looks perfectly sound. Just keep some liniment on those legs and give her a couple days' rest. I'll call you in about an hour with the results of the X rays."

Mike phoned Mr. Rosen to let him know what had happened, then they loaded Dreamer into the trailer and headed back to Edgardale. Despite Mike's words, Ashleigh couldn't help feeling she could have done something to stop Dreamer from getting herself into trouble. All the more reason for her to learn everything she possibly could about working with horses on the track. *If only I could go to that race camp,* she thought.

When they reached Edgardale, they found that the vet had already phoned to let them know Dreamer's X rays had come back clean. Ashleigh breathed a sigh of relief as she saddled her mare and prepared to ride to the Wortons'. She led Stardust from the barn and mounted up, cutting across the large field that separated their two properties. She found Mrs. Worton standing outside the barn when she arrived.

"Hello," the petite woman called when Ashleigh rode up. "What brings you here this afternoon?"

Ashleigh dismounted and unsnapped her helmet, pulling it from her head and tucking it under her arm. Now that she was here, she wasn't exactly sure what to say.

Mrs. Worton's eyes twinkled. "Did you come about the camp?"

Ashleigh nodded.

"I thought so." Mrs. Worton smiled and motioned for her to turn Stardust out in one of the holding pens outside the barn.

Ashleigh slipped off the mare's bridle and saddle, then followed the dark-haired woman into the barn.

"I'll grab the application form from the office," Mrs. Worton said.

Ashleigh paused in the middle of the barn aisle and cleared her throat nervously. "Uh, before you do that, I've got a question for you." She jammed her hands into her pockets and looked into the woman's kind brown eyes. She took a deep breath and began. "My parents said that with breeding season coming up, we don't really have the extra money to spend on the camp. I have a couple hundred dollars in my savings account. I was wondering if maybe you could give me a discount, and let me work the rest of the fee off by doing barn chores for you?"

Mrs. Worton lifted her eyebrows. "My goodness, Ashleigh, that would be a lot of stalls to clean." She shook her head. "If it were just up to me, I'd find a way to work something out with you. You've been a big help to us on several occasions. But this camp is going to cost us a lot of money, and we've got businesses sponsoring us. We need twenty fully paid students to make this work."

Ashleigh felt as though someone had punched her in the stomach. Her best idea had just failed, and she couldn't come up with another way to get into the camp.

Mrs. Worton put an arm around her shoulder and led her to the barn office. "Don't look so sad, Ash. These things have a way of working out. We've got several weeks left before camp starts. Maybe your parents will sell a yearling by then and you'll be able to come to camp." She opened the door to the office. "I was just putting together the tack boxes. Would you like to help?"

Ashleigh spied the shiny silver trunks and the piles of multicolored brushes and hoof picks, along with various saddles and bridles that lay scattered around the room. She nodded vigorously.

Mrs. Worton indicated a tack trunk that had already been put together. "I need to make up nine more boxes just like this one," she said. "Try to color-coordinate all the brushes so that the equipment in each tack box is the same color."

As Ashleigh worked, she tried not to think about how it would be somebody else getting to use all of this neat equipment. She reminded herself that she still had a few more weeks. Maybe a miracle would happen and she would get to go to camp after all.

On Monday morning Ashleigh hopped off the school bus and headed to her classroom. "Dreamer's legs are in great shape and her tendons are tight and cold," she told Mona. "She's in perfect shape for her upcoming race."

"That's great news," Mona said. "It would have been horrible if Dreamer got hurt before her racing career even began." She opened the door to the school. "Any more news on the race camp?" she asked.

Ashleigh frowned. "Only that it will take a miracle to get me into that camp," she said. She opened the door to the classroom and noticed several kids standing in the center of the room staring at the walls and ceiling. "What's going on? . . . Oh, gross!" Ashleigh gasped.

Mona stifled a giggle as they followed the glistening trails of slime up the walls from the lidless tank that used to house fifty large snails. The snails had migrated up the walls, and some of them were on the ceiling.

Ashleigh felt a finger jab into her back and heard the sound of the voice she dreaded.

"Better check your desk, Smashleigh," Vince warned. "There might be some extra snails in there."

Ashleigh bit her lip and walked to her desk, knowing that she would find the extra snails the bully had warned her about. She removed them with a grimace, put them back in their tank, and replaced the lid.

"Oh, dear!" their teacher, Mrs. Wilson, exclaimed when she entered the room. "I must have forgotten to replace the lid when I fed the snails on Friday."

Ashleigh's eyes cut quickly to where Vince sat at his desk, tipped back in his chair with a satisfied smirk on his face. She knew this was one of the bully's pranks, but she had no way to prove it. Unfortunately, Vince had gotten away with another mean trick.

"Don't let him get to you, Ash," Mona said. She placed her books on the desk next to Ashleigh's and turned her back to Vince. "Someday he's going to get in a lot of trouble."

Ashleigh took her seat and sighed. She tried to ignore Vince and concentrate on something else. A girl's voice cut into her thoughts, and Ashleigh's ears perked at the mention of the race camp.

"Molly and Gus are going," said Sybil, a girl with long blond hair who sat in the first row. "They're really excited."

Ashleigh felt a pang of jealousy, but she tried to tamp it down. Gus and Molly were nice kids; they deserved to go. But now the camp was two more spots closer to being filled, and Ashleigh wasn't any nearer to figuring out how she was going to get in.

Two weeks before race camp was to begin, Dreamer was finally entered in a race. Mike had hauled the filly to Turfway Park earlier that morning. Ashleigh rode to the track with her family and Mona.

The Griffens pulled into the parking lot on the front side of the racetrack, using a special parking pass Mike had given them. Ashleigh smiled as she and Mona and her family walked through the horsemen's entrance to the grandstands. Mr. Rosen, in his flamboyant manner, had reserved the Griffens a table in the Racing Club, with passes to have lunch at the Finish Line Buffet.

Ashleigh and Mona hit the lunch line as soon as they were seated. Dreamer was entered in the fourth race of the day, and they wanted to be down front when Mike brought the filly into the saddling paddock. They loaded their plates and ate as fast as they could, asking to be excused as soon as they were finished.

"Take Rory with you," Mrs. Griffen said. "And don't wander far from the saddling paddock and the winner's circle. We'll be down as soon as everyone else is finished with lunch."

Ashleigh grabbed Rory's hand and followed Mona down to where the horses were being saddled for the next race. Several Thoroughbreds were circling the walking ring with their grooms, while to the right of the ring, the rest of the horses were being saddled in the saddling stalls. In the center of the walking ring was a square brick platform. This was where the owners and trainers sat and waited for the call to the post.

When the fourth race arrived, Ashleigh pushed her way through the crowd by the saddling paddock to the number four stall, where the beautiful gray filly danced nervously as she was saddled. Satisfied that the filly was doing fine, Ashleigh turned to Mona and suggested, "Let's get to the rail before it gets too crowded so we can pick our spot near the finish line."

No sooner had the girls found a good spot than the rest of Ashleigh's family arrived, and they all crowded in on the length of railing closest to the finish line to watch the horses parade before the grandstand. Ashleigh was surprised when Mr. Rosen joined them on the rail.

Dreamer's owner turned to the tote board, where the odds for each horse were posted. "Ten to one." He made a tsking sound as he rubbed his bald spot. "If it wasn't for that gallop boy letting this filly get away from him a couple weeks ago, Dreamer would be going off at twenty-to-one odds and I'd be a whole lot richer after she wins." He shook his head in disgust and left to place his bet.

"Is money all he ever thinks about?" Mona asked.

Ashleigh nodded. "Money and fame," she said. "You should see him puff up when the reporters come around."

The horses finished the post parade and cantered to the other side of the one-mile track, where they would load in the starting gate for their six-furlong race.

While they waited for the horses to load, Ashleigh and Mona checked out the inside of the racecourse. Just beyond the tote board was a lake, now partially iced over from the wintry weather, and from where they stood, they could just make out the show ring next to the barns, where jumping and horse shows took place during the summer.

The announcer's voice boomed over the speaker system. "The horses are now being loaded for the running of the fourth race of the day."

Mr. Rosen returned and pushed his way to the

front of the crowd. Ashleigh barely missed getting her toes stepped on. She thought about squeezing back into the spot that she'd just been pushed out of, but she caught a warning look from her mother and decided against it.

"The last horse is being loaded into the starting gate," the announcer said. "And they're off!"

Ashleigh stood on her toes, craning her neck to see where Dreamer was. It didn't take her long to find the filly in the herd of battling horses. Dreamer was in the lead as the field ran up the back side of the dirt track, her easy stride carrying her to an even bigger lead by the time she reached the turn.

Mike looked at the fractions on the tote board. "She ran the first quarter in twenty-one and change," he said in amazement. "That's awfully fast. I'm not sure she'll be able to keep up that pace."

"Dream Time leads by six lengths, with Battle Born a distant second, and Holy Holly coming on in third," the announcer called.

Ashleigh watched as they came out of the final turn and Dreamer switched leads for the straight run down the homestretch. Jack tipped his whip but didn't touch the filly with it. Instead he leaned low and pushed his hands up her neck, urging her to give it everything she had. Despite the fast early fractions, Dreamer pinned her ears and opened up her lead even more, pulling ahead by ten lengths in the final furlong before the finish line.

"It's Dream Time all alone at the finish line!" the announcer cried above the roar of the ecstatic crowd.

"She did it!" Ashleigh hollered as she jumped up and down and hugged Mona. "And she made it look so easy!"

Mike herded everyone toward the winner's circle. "Did you see the final time? Dreamer was only a fraction off the track record!"

Jonathan Rosen puffed out his chest and flashed his winning tickets. "I knew she'd do it," he crowed. "I've got the proof right here!"

Ashleigh rolled her eyes. This was Dreamer's special moment. She hoped Mr. Rosen would be quiet about winning his big bet and let people focus on the filly and her talented jockey.

Several reporters crowded next to the winner's circle. "Mr. Rosen," one of them called, "I'm from the *Daily Racing Form*. I'd like to interview you about Dream Time when you're finished with your win photo."

Mr. Rosen smiled broadly for their cameras. "I'll be with you in just a minute, gentlemen." He beamed and slicked his hair over his bald spot.

Ashleigh glanced at Mona and shook her head. "He looks like a rooster, puffing up his feathers!"

Mona laughed and nodded in agreement. They stepped back when the big filly was led into the winner's circle and positioned for the photo.

Ashleigh reached out to touch the sweating filly's hot neck. "You did great, girl!" she praised the horse.

Dreamer bobbed her head and craned her neck to give Ashleigh a nudge with her nose.

Jack Dale looked down at Ashleigh and winked. "I can definitely tell who this filly favors." He laughed. "I hope you're staying on as her favorite groom."

"Oh, yes," Ashleigh replied as she smiled at the winning jockey with stars in her eyes. "Dreamer trains at our farm. I spend as much time with her as I can." She saw the confused look pass across the jockey's face, and a funny feeling ricocheted through her stomach. Did Mr. Rosen have other plans for Dreamer?

Jack took off his helmet for the win photo, but he turned back to Ashleigh after the blinding lights flashed. "Mr. Rosen told me he was moving the filly back to the track before her next race."

All the happiness Ashleigh felt from the win drained out of her at the news. Dreamer was being taken away from Edgardale!

The official win sign flashed on the tote board, and

Dreamer jumped as the crowd roared their approval. Ashleigh put a steadying hand on the filly's neck, feeling Dreamer's muscles quake beneath her palm. Ashleigh's stomach knotted. Dreamer was so high-strung. Would she survive training at the busy racetrack? Or would the distractions of living in such a busy environment be the filly's undoing?

One thing was for sure—if Dreamer moved to the racetrack, Ashleigh wouldn't be able to help the filly on a daily basis. She took a deep breath and sighed. Without race camp or Dreamer to fill her days, how was she going to while away the long winter months?

The following day Mike arrived with his trailer to take Dreamer to the track. Ashleigh slipped the leather halter over the filly's head and threw her arms about the animal's neck, breathing in the warm horse scent. "I'm going to miss you," she said, choking back the tears. Stardust nickered, and Ashleigh smiled. "See, she's going to miss you, too." Dreamer nuzzled her cheek, and Ashleigh felt the tears trickle down her face.

Mike poked his head into the stall. "It's time to load up," he said.

Ashleigh wiped the dampness from her face and

turned to the trainer. "I don't understand why Mr. Rosen is taking Dreamer away when he knows that Edgardale is the best place for her to train."

Mike nodded in agreement. "I tried to talk some sense into him, but he wouldn't listen. He threatened to send Dreamer to another trainer if I didn't take her to the racetrack to train. He wants this filly where the press can take lots of photos and write stories about her." He shrugged. "There's nothing I can do except go along and hope that I can eventually talk some sense into him."

Mike smiled at Ashleigh in sympathy. "I know how much you like Dreamer, Ash. The filly will be racing again in a week. I'll swing by and pick you up next Saturday if it's okay with your parents. At least you can see the filly on weekends." He paused. "That is, unless you get into your race camp. Then you'll probably be too busy."

Ashleigh gave the trainer a tremulous smile. "I'd like to go to the track with you for Dreamer's next race. I'll talk to my parents about it."

She turned back to the gray filly. "You'll be fine, Dreamer," she said speaking past the lump in her throat. "Just ignore all the distractions at the track, and you'll do great."

They loaded the filly, and Ashleigh watched the

trailer rumble down Edgardale's driveway with a heavy feeling in her heart. She was going to miss Dreamer terribly. She felt a reassuring hand on her shoulder and turned to see her parents standing beside her.

"She's a pretty special filly," Mr. Griffen said.

Ashleigh nodded in agreement. She watched the truck and trailer until they pulled out of sight, then turned to her parents. "Why would somebody do something that they know wasn't good for the horse?" she asked.

Mr. Griffen removed his hat and dusted it on his jeans. "Mr. Rosen is the kind of man who puts his own wants before the needs of his animals," he said in dismay. "It's a sad fact that there are people like that and, worse yet, that there's nothing you can do about it." He put his arms around his wife and daughter and steered them toward the house. "Let's just hope everything works out for the best. We'll simply have to be content to watch Dreamer race, and maybe visit her from time to time at the track."

Ashleigh tried to feel content with that, but she couldn't. Dreamer belonged at Edgardale. She had one more week until she could see the filly again, and a few more days after that to find a way to get to race camp. The big block of time in between would be filled with nothing but school. Ashleigh frowned. Her situation was looking worse by the moment. At least she had Stardust to ride; she had to be grateful for that.

Ashleigh closed her spelling book when the bell rang. She quickly packed her things away and left the classroom, not bothering to scan the halls for Vince before she entered them. It had been at least a week since she'd had a run-in with the rude boy. *Maybe Vince has found somebody else to pick on,* she thought.

Ashleigh whistled happily as she moved through the crowded hallway preparing to leave the school. She met up with Mona on the bus.

"What are you so happy about?" Mona asked as she slid into the seat beside Ashleigh. "Did you figure a way to get into race camp?"

Ashleigh grinned. "I'd be doing somersaults if that were true. No, I'm happy because I haven't had any Vince problems lately."

Mona pulled off her gloves and put them in her jacket pockets. "What about all the rats that were let out of their cages in Mr. Jones's science class?"

Ashleigh settled back in her seat and chuckled. "That was definitely a Vince prank, but at least he didn't put one of the rats in my book bag." She knocked on the bus window and waved to Jamie and Lynne as they walked past.

"Dream Time is running this weekend," Jamie called through the closed window. "Are you going to Turfway Park?"

Ashleigh nodded. Her parents had agreed to take her to Turfway to watch the filly run her second race. She had been following the stories in the *Daily Racing Form*. Dreamer's next race was a small stakes, but the field was loaded with fillies that were pointed toward much bigger races such as the Breeders' Cup series and the Mother Goose Stakes. This race would definitely be a proving ground for Dreamer.

Ashleigh buried herself in homework and barn chores, trying to make the time pass quickly. When Saturday finally arrived, she jumped out of bed before anyone else in the house had risen and made her way to the barn to start her chores. She was surprised to discover a light dusting of snow on the ground when she left the house. She donned her mittens and pulled her stocking cap low over her ears.

Jonas was mixing the morning grain when she entered the big brown barn. "Good morning, Jonas," she called to the burly stable hand as he bent over the grain box, scooping out rations.

Jonas grunted. "It sure is a cold morning," he said as his breath frosted the air. "I hope it warms up for today's races. That track's going to be mighty hard for those fine-boned Thoroughbreds to be pounding across."

Ashleigh picked up the first set of feed buckets and carried them to the broodmares' stalls. "Mike will scratch Dreamer if he thinks the track's too hard," she assured Jonas. "He won't take a chance on hurting the filly." She finished feeding the horses, then set to work cleaning stalls. It wasn't long before her parents made their way down to the barn. Rory and Caroline followed twenty minutes later, and the entire family worked to complete the morning chores.

When she was finished, Ashleigh put away the wheelbarrow and made her way to the house. The rumble of a big truck on the main road made her turn and look. Even from this distance, she could see that the vehicle was a large horse van. She followed its progress as it slowed in front of the Wortons' farm and pulled into their driveway.

Ashleigh pulled off her muck boots and thought about the horses in the van. She was sure they were being delivered for the race camp, which was scheduled to begin in a week. She wondered what kind of horses they were. Would they be stakes horses or cheap claimers? She opened the door to the house and sighed. At this point she shouldn't even care. The closer they got to the first day of camp, the further away her dream of attending the camp seemed to be.

She hung her coat on the hook in the hallway and concentrated on the day ahead. Dreamer was going to win her second race! She got ready as fast as she could and was the first one to the car.

Ashleigh played the alphabet game with Rory to make the trip seem shorter. By the time she had purposely let him beat her at least twice, they were pulling onto the back side of the track. Ashleigh signed in at the security gate while the rest of her family made their way to the cafeteria for a bite to eat. She just wanted to check on Dreamer before she ate lunch.

She cut through the front barns, admiring the shed rows that were decorated with plants and racing colors. She wondered how the grooms managed to get flowers to survive in this cold temperature, but on closer inspection, she learned that the flowers were made of silk.

As she neared Mike's tack room, she heard the sound of angry voices coming from within. Mike and Mr. Rosen seemed to be in a heated discussion. She paused in front of Dreamer's stall, which was just outside the tack-room door, and eavesdropped on the conversation while she patted the gray filly.

"I'm telling you, Jonathan." Mike's voice had a desperate edge to it. "The track is too hard. It's partially frozen, and it's just not worth the risk. Dreamer has to be scratched from this race!"

"Come on, Mike," Mr. Rosen answered in a placating tone. "This is the type of fast track that records can be set on. Dreamer was so close to the track record on her first outing. I know she can break the record today."

"She could also get hurt," Mike said angrily. "Did you think of that? It was only a couple of weeks ago that Dreamer got her legs caught over that hotwalker arm. I know her X rays came back clean, but a hard track like the one out there today could make any weak spot worse," he explained. "I'm going to the office to scratch her. It's simply not worth taking a chance on hurting this filly."

Ashleigh stepped back as the door swung open and the two men emerged. Mr. Rosen looked her up and down, nodded curtly, and turned back to the trainer.

"The X rays came back clean because there's *nothing there,*" Mr. Rosen said. "Dreamer is *my* horse. There are a lot of reporters here today to watch Dreamer set a new record, and I will not disappoint them. You *will* run Dreamer in this stakes race today, and tomorrow I will be looking for a new trainer!" Mr. Rosen declared, and stomped off down the shed row.

Ashleigh stroked her hand down Dreamer's face, kissing her on her soft black-tipped muzzle. "What are you going to do, Mike?" She looked worriedly toward the trainer. "Could Dreamer really get hurt out there today?"

Mike ran an anxious hand through his hair. "The truth is, she could get hurt anytime she goes out onto the track," the older man said. "That's part of racing, Ashleigh. These are very large animals with delicate legs, and they're running at very fast speeds. That compounds the risk to those legs. That's why we take our time conditioning these Thoroughbreds and getting them ready to race. Training a horse properly cuts down on its chances of breaking down," he explained. "But racing on a track that's partially frozen is risking more than we need to."

"But aren't other trainers running their horses today?" Ashleigh asked.

Mike nodded. "A lot of the trainers will still run today. But many have already scratched their horses. I think we should be one of them. This filly is worth too much to take the chance of hurting her," he said. "She's got plenty of races left in her. Why the rush?"

Ashleigh scowled. "Because Mr. Rosen likes being in the spotlight," she said. "How can an owner be like that? How can he care more about publicity and cashing in on a bet then he does about his horse?"

Mike reached out and ruffled Ashleigh's hair. "That's why you're so great with horses," he said proudly. "You care." He glanced at his watch. "I bet your parents are up getting a bite to eat. Why don't you go grab a quick lunch and meet me back here in half an hour? You can help me get Dreamer ready for her race, since Mr. Rosen has his heart set on running her."

Ashleigh nodded and headed back to the cafeteria. She couldn't wait to discuss the race with her parents. She cut down the barn aisles and wound her way back to the track's kitchen. Her parents were just starting their lunch when she arrived. She related the story about Dreamer, and just as she had suspected, her parents sided with Mike.

"Mr. Rosen is the worst kind of owner," Mrs. Griffen said. "He's paying Mike to do a job. He should value Mike's opinion and let him do that job."

Mr. Griffen nodded in agreement as he spread some mustard on his sandwich. "When we're finished here, we'll go help Mike ready the filly for the race, then we'll drive over to the front side." He saw the disappointed look on his daughter's face. "I know you were looking forward to walking over with Dreamer, Ash, but I think we need to stay out of Mr. Rosen's way. This matter is between him and Mike."

Ashleigh ate the bowl of chicken noodle soup her parents had gotten for her. The warm broth felt good after being outside in the cold. When they finished their meal, they went to help Mike prepare the filly, then drove to the front side of the racetrack to await the start of the race.

"There's Mr. Rosen." Derek Griffen pointed to the bricked area in the middle of the saddling ring, where Dreamer's owner stood talking to reporters.

Ashleigh looked on in disgust as the big man crowed for the press.

The noise of the crowd grew, and Ashleigh knew that the horses for Dreamer's race were arriving. The elegant gray pranced into the saddling paddock with her neck bowed. The crowd murmured their approval. Ashleigh couldn't help but smile. The filly was so beautiful! Dreamer's dapples stood out a darker gray than the rest of her coat, showing her good health. Ashleigh had brushed the filly's black mane and tail until they gleamed. There were some high-class fillies in this race, but Ashleigh thought Dreamer was the prettiest of them all.

When all the horses were saddled, the bell rang, calling the jockeys to the saddling paddock. Ashleigh flushed with pleasure when Jack Dale smiled and waved to her.

"I'm going to get you another win photo today, little lady," he said as he gave her a thumbs-up sign. Then he went to get his riding instructions from Mike.

Ashleigh noticed that Mr. Rosen cut in on what Mike was saying to the jockey, and Mike didn't look the least bit pleased about it. His mouth formed a grim line as he legged up the jockey and walked the horse out of the ring to the waiting pony rider.

"Is everything all right?" Mr. Griffen asked when they joined Mike by the rail for the post parade and he saw the angry expression on the trainer's face.

Mike shook his head in disgust. "This filly shouldn't be racing today, but since she is, I was asking the jockey to take it easy on her. Mr. Rosen overheard and gave explicit instructions that Jack was to go for the record. It's out of my hands now," he said.

The post parade ended, and the horses cantered to the back side of the racetrack, where the starting gate stood at the six-furlong mark. Mr. Rosen was several yards away from where the Griffens and Mike stood, but Ashleigh could hear the owner bragging about Dreamer and all the money she was going to make him. He was bragging so much that a big cloud of frozen breath hung in the air above his head. Ashleigh frowned and turned away, waiting for the race to begin.

The race announcer's voice broke over the hum of the crowd. "The horses are loading in the gate for the running of today's sixth race, a stakes race for three-year-old fillies."

"Here we go." Mike leaned on the rail, waiting for the gate to pop.

"They're off and running!" the announcer cried. "Dream Time breaks on top and takes her position on the inside rail. Thunder's Pride is second, and Leah's Hope is moving up to challenge."

"Look at her go!" Mr. Rosen hollered as he joined the others at the rail. "Look at that first-quarter fraction!" He pointed to the tote board. "She's definitely going to break the record if she keeps that pace up."

Ashleigh stood on her toes as the horses moved into the turn and Dreamer opened up another five lengths on the pack. "Can she keep up that speed?" she asked Mike.

The trainer nodded grimly. "Let's hope so," he said.

The announcer's voice blared above the roar of the crowd as the horses rounded the turn and pounded down the homestretch. "It's Dream Time running away from the rest of the pack, opening her lead to fifteen lengths! We could see a new record here today at Turfway Park, folks!"

Ashleigh's breath caught in her throat when she saw the filly bobble slightly at the sixteenth pole. The move was so small, she wasn't sure she had actually seen it, but Mike tensed beside her.

Dream Time lined out and continued to run for the finish line, but she was no longer pulling away from the rest of the horses. Ashleigh could see the others were gaining on her, but Dreamer's lead was so wide, it would be impossible for them to catch her at this point.

The speedy gray pinned her ears and pumped her pistonlike legs, driving for the finish line, but several strides before the wire, she bobbled again and her gait changed noticeably. Dream Time crossed the finish line first, and Mr. Rosen whooped for joy, thrusting his fistful of winning tickets above his head. "I told you she could do it!" he crowed to Mike. "She didn't break the record, but she sure won like a champion! Guess you were wrong about wanting to scratch her today," he said as he slapped Mike on the back.

Ashleigh ignored the boastful owner and kept her eyes glued to the filly, knowing that something wasn't right.

The jockey stood in the irons and gathered the big

gray, trying to hold her together. Just as the other horses caught up to them, Dream Time stumbled hard, and it was obvious that she was hurt badly. She pulled herself up within a few strides, and Jack jumped out of the saddle before the filly came to a full halt.

"You can stop braying like a donkey," Mike said to Mr. Rosen, anxiously surveying the scene. "Your horse is hurt, and it doesn't look good from here." Then he took off at a run.

Ashleigh followed closely on the trainer's heels, hoping that Dreamer had just thrown a shoe. But as the crowd of grooms and trainers parted from where they stood around the valiant filly, Ashleigh could see that the situation was much, much worse than that.

4

The cold air burned in and out of her lungs as Ashleigh raced down the track behind Mike. Her father had come with her to help, and she could hear his steady breathing and the clomp of his boots as he kept pace behind her.

Dreamer has to be okay! She willed it to be true. But when they reached the spot where the filly stood ringed by riders and grooms who were trying to keep her from moving, Ashleigh could see the pain on the sweet filly's face as she held her front right leg in the air. Her sides still heaved from the race, and foam flecked her neck. The jockey removed his tack and stroked the filly's neck, speaking calming words while he waited for Mike to reach them.

The track veterinarian arrived at the same time. Mike took Dreamer's reins from the jockey and motioned for him to get back to the weigh-in. Even though Dreamer was hurt, she had crossed the finish line first with her rider in the irons. If Jack didn't weigh in, Dreamer would be disqualified from winning the race.

"Is it a bowed tendon, Doc?" Mike craned his neck to look over the vet's shoulder.

Dr. Danner shook his head and hollered for his assistant. "Get the horse ambulance! Make it quick!"

Ashleigh felt the blood run cold in her veins. Horses that were picked up in the ambulance trailer were often taken to the machine yard to be put down. "What is it?" She crowded close to the vet. "What's the matter with Dreamer?"

Dr. Danner looked to Mike. "Do you want the girl to see this?"

Ashleigh choked on a breath. She commanded her lungs to fill, but she couldn't seem to get any air. She gasped and focused on the veterinarian. If she didn't pull herself together, they would make her leave. She wanted to be with Dreamer. The filly needed her now more than ever.

Mike nodded to the vet. "Ashleigh's been Dreamer's number one groom. As long as her father says it's okay, she can stay."

Ashleigh turned beseeching eyes on her father, begging him not to send her away.

Mr. Griffen put a hand on her shoulder. "This might be rough, Ash. Are you sure you want to?"

Ashleigh bobbed her head furiously. She didn't trust her voice enough to speak.

Several horses returning to the unsaddling area trotted past, and Dream Time tossed her head and began to struggle. She attempted to put weight on the leg and almost fell.

"Easy, easy," Mike crooned as he put a steadying hand on the filly's neck, trying to calm her. "Did she pull the ligaments?" the trainer asked.

The vet stood and frowned. "It looks like a bad fracture, Mike. She'll probably have to be put down. You'd better contact her owner."

Ashleigh felt the world tilt, and specks of gray dotted her vision. She felt her father reach out to steady her, but she wasn't at all sure her legs would hold her. Put down? That wasn't possible! The filly had just won her second race. How could they be talking about destroying her? There had to be some way to save her.

"Here's Mr. Rosen now," Mike said.

Jonathan Rosen huffed and puffed from his awkward jog up the track. "What's going on here? We've got a win photo to pose for. I've got win tickets to cash."

Ashleigh wanted to push the pompous man down on his big backside. The vet was talking about putting

Dreamer to sleep, and all Mr. Rosen could think about was getting his picture taken and cashing in on his bets.

"The filly's hurt bad, Jonathan," Mike said. "The vet needs your permission to have her destroyed."

Mr. Rosen's jaw went slack. "Destroyed? Dreamer just won her first two races. She's got a whole career in front of her. What do you mean, she needs to be put down?"

Dr. Danner pointed to the injured leg. "The cannon bone has a bad fracture, sir. There's a small possibility of saving her, but it's very, very rough for the horse. I'm recommending that you have the filly put down."

Mr. Rosen rubbed his chin. "She'll never run again?" he said in dismay. "Well, if she can't run, then she's not worth anything." He stood for a moment, and then, with a nod of his head, gave the vet permission to have the filly destroyed.

Ashleigh could stand it no longer. How could the man be so callous? There had to be a way to save Dreamer. "Wait!" she cried, and stepped forward. "There's got to be something you could do to save her! Dreamer could be a great broodmare if you'll just let her live!" She saw the doubtful look on Mr. Rosen's face. She knew the only way to get through to the man was with money or fame. She tried another approach.

"Dreamer could have babies that would sell for a lot of money. Maybe one of them could win the Derby."

That got Mr. Rosen's attention. "You think she'd be a good broodmare?" he asked, looking straight at Mr. Griffen.

Derek Griffen nodded. "I wish I had a filly like her in my broodmare barn," he said. "She's got great bloodlines, and we know she can run. This is the kind of mare every breeder hopes to get hold of. Her foals will bring a lot of money at the sale."

Ashleigh smiled gratefully at her father, then held her breath, waiting for Mr. Rosen's response.

Mr. Rosen paused for a moment, then nodded. "Okay, we'll give it a try."

Ashleigh let out the breath she was holding. The cold air carried it off like smoke. "Thanks, Dad," she whispered, and squeezed his hand.

Dr. Danner gave the filly a big dose of painkiller. The horse ambulance arrived, and Ashleigh almost wished she hadn't stayed to watch. Dreamer tried to do what was asked of her, but loading into a trailer on three legs—especially when she was sedated—was very difficult for her.

Dr. Danner approached Mike. "The operation's going to take several hours. We'll have to do it here on the grounds. I can't risk hauling her all the way to the hospital. If she goes down in the trailer, that will be the end of it."

Mike nodded. "We'll wait in the cafeteria."

The next several hours were the longest Ashleigh had ever spent. The clock seemed to be moving backward. She tried playing cards with her father, but she couldn't concentrate. She watched the rest of the races on television and read through an entire pile of *Daily Racing Forms*. Finally Dr. Danner's assistant came to get them.

"She'll be coming out of the anesthetic pretty soon," the young man said. "Dr. Danner would like the owner there when the filly wakes up."

They found Mr. Rosen and went to the stall where the operation had been performed.

Ashleigh peeked over the door. Dreamer lay flat out on her side with a white cast on her right leg that ran from her ankle to her knee.

"The operation went fine," Dr. Danner assured them. "The most delicate part will be when she comes out of the anesthesia. She'll need to be kept quiet for a while."

Mr. Rosen peeked in at the unconscious filly. "She sure doesn't look like a winner now, does she?" he said hollowly.

Ashleigh opened her mouth to say something, but

her mother clamped a hand on her shoulder, warning her to keep silent. Ashleigh crossed her arms and fumed. If the owner had listened to Mike's advice and not run the filly on the frozen track, Dreamer wouldn't be in this situation. How could an owner be so cruel and uncaring?

Dr. Danner stepped into the stall. "She's starting to come around." He moved to the mare's side. "Easy, girl," he said in soft, reassuring tones, but the filly came to her senses quickly and began to panic in the unfamiliar surroundings.

Dream Time flopped in the thick bed of straw, banging her head and legs against the floor as she struggled to rise.

"Whoa, easy!" Dr. Danner cried as he tried to calm the mare. "Greg, get in here!" he called to his assistant.

Mike ran into the stall with the vet's assistant. "What can I do?" he asked.

Dr. Danner placed his hands on the filly's broad cheekbone and neck. "Help me hold her head down so she can't stand up. Greg, get me a sedative, quick!"

Dreamer groaned, and the sound of her ragged breaths filled the cement-block stall as she thrashed about. Ashleigh clutched the front of her jacket, willing the filly to lie still, but Dreamer continued to struggle. "Please hold still, Dreamer," she whispered.

The assistant handed a syringe to the vet, and Dr. Danner administered the tranquilizer. Dreamer groaned several more times, then lay still on the golden bed of straw.

Ashleigh held her breath. “Is she dead?” she squeaked in a very small voice.

Mike and Dr. Danner rose from the stall floor. The vet shook his head. “No, she’s only sleeping, but this episode wasn’t good. I’ll have to X-ray that leg to make sure the screws held.” He motioned for his assistant to get the portable X-ray machine. “I can have these developed at the hospital down the road,” he said. “It’ll take at least another hour, folks.”

Ashleigh plopped down on a bale of straw that sat outside Dreamer’s stall. She wasn’t going anywhere until she heard the news. Mr. Rosen sat down beside her, and Ashleigh scooted over to the far side of the bale.

“This is going to cost me a fortune!” Mr. Rosen grouched. “It’ll take every penny of what Dreamer earned in those last two races, and then some.” He rose and went to pour himself a cup of hot coffee from the vet’s on-site office down the way.

Dr. Danner left the stall with the new X rays in his hand. “Let’s hope these show there’s no more damage,” he said.

Mr. Griffen stood and shook the vet’s other hand.

"You've done a great job, Doc. Dreamer was stabled at Edgardale, and we've become rather fond of her." He pointed to Ashleigh. "Especially my daughter, Ashleigh. She was very close to the filly."

Ashleigh swallowed the lump in her throat and asked the question no one else would ask. "What happens if there's more damage?"

Dr. Danner smiled kindly at her. "Well, Ashleigh," the veterinarian began, "the problem with broken legs is that horses don't have very good circulation in their lower extremities. That's why a horse's legs are always cold to the touch if it's sound. Unfortunately, that also makes for difficult healing if something breaks below the knee." The vet ran a tired hand through his hair and stared at the adults. "I'm afraid if she's undone the repair, I'm going to recommend that the filly be put down."

Everyone sat in stunned silence, listening to the echo of the vet's footfalls as he walked away. They waited for his return for almost an hour. When Dr. Danner finally arrived, Ashleigh knew by the grim set of the vet's jaw that the news wasn't good.

"What is it, Doc?" Mike asked.

The vet blew an exhausted sigh. "I'm afraid two of the screws we set have come undone. They can be reset, but the chances are that when the filly comes out of the anesthetic again, she'll do the same thing."

"How much is this costing me?" Mr. Rosen asked as he joined the group gathered around the vet.

Dr. Danner eyed the man with disdain. "I don't need to tell you the bill is already quite high."

Mr. Rosen shoved his hands into his pockets and grunted. "I can't afford to throw good money after bad," he said. "I'm sitting on a big vet bill now—which will double if we operate again—and we could get the exact same result. And I still owe Mike for two months' worth of training." He paused and stared at the prone filly. "Put her down." He turned and walked down the aisle away from everyone.

"Wait!" Ashleigh cried, jumping to her feet. "She still has a chance. You can't do this to Dreamer!" She choked on a sob and turned to her parents. "Please don't let them do this. We can save Dreamer. I know we can! We can move her to Edgardale, where she knows everyone. I'll stay will her night and day and make sure she doesn't move and hurt her leg. She trusts me!"

Mr. Griffen turned to the vet. "Is there a chance the filly could make it?"

The vet shrugged. "There's always a chance."

Ashleigh wiped at the tears that flowed freely down her cheeks. "We could buy Dreamer from Mr. Rosen. He doesn't want her."

Mrs. Griffen hugged her daughter to her. "I wish it

were that easy, Ash. But we don't have the money for the mare or the operation."

Mike called after the owner, "Just a second, Jonathan." He turned to the Griffens. "I might be able to help."

Mr. Rosen returned and stared curiously.

"The Griffens would like to buy Dreamer," he said.

Mr. Rosen's eyebrows drew to a point. "You'd pay good money for a horse that the vet thinks won't make it?" He was flabbergasted, then grew curious. "How much are you willing to pay for a horse that's almost dead?"

Mr. Griffen pulled the hat from his head and twisted it in his hands. "The truth is—" he began, but was cut off by the trainer.

"I owe the Griffens," Mike said as he looked over his shoulder, warning them to let him talk. "I'd be willing to cancel my training bill on Dream Time in return for the filly."

Now Mr. Rosen was really perplexed. "You'd throw away that kind of money on a horse that's half dead?" He tossed his hands in the air and laughed. "I can't lose on this offer. You've got yourself a deal! And good riddance to all of you fools!" He puffed out his chest, pleased with the exchange, and walked down the shed row, laughing as he went.

Ashleigh felt anger rolling within her. She didn't think she had ever despised anyone as much as Jonathan Rosen. His careless decision had wrecked a perfectly good horse. But at least the filly was out of his hands now. He couldn't hurt her anymore.

"Thank you, Mike," Mr. Griffen said. "That was a very kind thing you just did."

They only had one more hurdle left to clear—the vet bill, which Ashleigh knew would be beyond their means.

Dr. Danner came to the rescue. He placed a fatherly hand on Ashleigh's head. "You remind me so much of my Susan," he said. "She's a little older than you are, but just as horse-crazy." He looked from Mike to the Griffens. "If you're really serious about saving this filly, I'll make you a deal."

Everyone listened in rapt attention as the vet explained the situation. "Mr. Rosen is responsible for the bill on the first operation," Dr. Danner said. "If Dream Time survives the second operation, I'll wait and take my fees after you sell her first foal. If she doesn't make it, I'll volunteer my time and only charge you for the cost of the supplies."

Mr. Griffen shook the vet's hand while Mrs. Griffen wiped a tear from her eye. Ashleigh hugged both Mike and the veterinarian.

"You might want to call your own vet," Dr. Danner suggested. "Right now I think our best hope is to do the surgery and put her in the trailer to Edgardale while she's still under."

Ashleigh perked up. "How can you do that while she's still asleep?" she asked curiously.

Dr. Danner grinned. "Believe me, there'll be a lot of sore backs around here tomorrow."

Ashleigh smiled briefly, but the sadness returned like a dark cloud hovering over her heart. Dreamer was coming back to Edgardale, but she was only a shadow of her former self.

"Boy, what a difference a day makes," Jonas said as he peered over the stall door to where Ashleigh knelt in the straw beside the unconscious filly.

Ashleigh ran a caring hand over the gray's soft coat and frowned. Jonas was right. Less than twenty-four hours before, Dreamer had been happily munching her oats at Turfway Park. And now she had been reduced to a broken-down horse whose life still hung in the balance.

The high-pitched neigh of one of their yearlings echoed across the pasture. Ashleigh thought about the Edgardale foals that were auctioned through the Keeneland sale each year. Was it worth all the time and effort they took to raise and care for their foals if they might end up seriously injured like Dreamer? Three years wasn't a very long time to live.

She thought about the race camp. It was only a week away. Was there anything they could teach her there that would help future owners and trainers to avoid catastrophes like this? In light of Dreamer's accident, the camp didn't seem so appealing anymore.

Maybe she was just tired. Ashleigh rubbed her temples, trying to massage away the ache that was settling there. For as long as she could remember, she had known she would follow in her parents' footsteps and have a career that involved racing Thoroughbreds—as a jockey, she hoped. But this day she was seeing another side of racing. She knew that horses sometimes were injured. But seeing a bad injury firsthand was more disconcerting than she had expected—especially when this one might have been prevented.

Dreamer groaned as she began to come out of the anesthetic. Ashleigh snapped to attention and called for her parents. Dr. Frankel, Edgardale's vet of many years, followed her parents into the stall.

"What can we do, Doc?" Mr. Griffen asked.

Dr. Frankel looked up. "I think I'll have everyone wait outside so the filly won't be alarmed if she comes to and sees a bunch of people standing around." He motioned to Ashleigh. "Since Dreamer is fond of you, it might help if you stay in the stall and talk to her quietly. It's very important that the filly remain calm when the tranquilizer wears off. That's where she got into trouble the first time." He stared intently at Ashleigh, trying to convey the importance of the situation. "We need Dreamer to stay calm and rest in the straw, or get up with a minimal amount of movement."

Ashleigh nodded solemnly. She understood that Dr. Frankel was trying to tell her that she was Dreamer's last hope. If she could keep the filly calm, Dreamer would have a good chance of making it. But what if she couldn't keep Dreamer from panicking? She swallowed hard, but the lump stayed in her throat.

Dr. Frankel gave her an encouraging smile. "Ashleigh, I want you to stand over by the door, close to Dreamer's head," he instructed. "If things go badly, I want you out of here quickly, and your parents can come into the stall to help. Do you understand?"

Ashleigh nodded. Dreamer's muscles began to twitch, and she groaned again. It was a painful sound, and it tore at Ashleigh's heart. She hunkered down beside the injured Thoroughbred and waited.

It seemed as though an eternity passed while they waited for the filly to come around. Ashleigh's legs felt as though they were being pricked by a million tiny needles. She shifted uneasily in the straw and bit her lip nervously. Dreamer began to groan in time with her exhaled breaths.

"She's waking up," the vet cautioned. "Ashleigh, start talking. We've got to keep this filly calm."

"Good girl. Just be quiet and soon you'll feel better again." Ashleigh wasn't even sure what words were coming out of her mouth. She only knew that they were some of the most important words she had ever spoken. She kept her voice low and rambled on about rides and races and all the foals that the beautiful gray filly was going to have. She stroked Dreamer's fine-boned face and delicate muzzle, whispering words of encouragement as the filly slowly drifted out of the sedative fog and into wakefulness.

The filly grunted loudly and raised her head. "Easy, girl. That's a good girl," Ashleigh crooned softly as she continued to stroke Dreamer's head and neck. She glanced at the vet for advice, but he just smiled and nodded.

"You're doing fine, Ashleigh," he said.

Dreamer heaved a heavy sigh and lay back in the straw, breathing deeply as her ears twitched and she gazed around the stall, trying to get her bearings. With a big grunt, she rolled into an upright position and lay with her injured leg extended in front of her.

"That's a good girl," Ashleigh said. As she continued her stream of words, she finger-brushed the tangles from the Thoroughbred's black mane.

Dr. Frankel slowly stepped over to the filly, extending his fingers so she could get the smell of him. He placed a quieting hand under her chin and massaged her lower jawbone. "I think we just cleared our first hurdle." He smiled at everyone present.

Ashleigh felt like jumping up and cheering, but instead, she shared the quiet victory with everyone by exchanging smiles.

"What now?" Mrs. Griffen asked.

Dr. Frankel slowly let himself and Ashleigh out of the stall. "I'll give her an injection of tranquilizer in her hindquarters," he answered. "That will take longer to get into her system, and will act more as a calming agent than a knockout drug. I'll leave several doses here for you to administer over the next several days. That will be a long enough time for her to adjust to her situation."

Ashleigh peeked over the door into Dreamer's stall. The filly was resting with her nose in the straw, still seemingly unaware of most of the things going on about her. "What happens when she tries to stand?"

Dr. Frankel rubbed his chin. "That will be our next hurdle. Dr. Danner put a full leg cast on to try to keep the entire leg immobilized for the time being. The pain should keep Dreamer from putting any weight on that leg. But if she starts floundering around trying to rise . . ."

Everyone knew the meaning of the unfinished sentence.

Mr. Griffen dropped his arm over Ashleigh's shoulders and gave her a hug. "You did a great job, kiddo. I'm proud of you." He gave her a nudge in the direction of the house. "The sun's gone down, and it's starting to get pretty cold. We'll finish up here."

"What about tonight?" Ashleigh asked in concern. "I want to spend the night in the barn in case something happens."

Mr. Griffen ruffled her hair. "That's what we've got a hired hand for," he teased. "Jonas will watch Dreamer tonight."

Ashleigh lifted her chin and looked her father directly in the eye. "But Dreamer trusts me. She's calmer when I'm around. Please let me stay the night with her. She needs me."

Mrs. Griffen touched her husband's arm. "It's a weekend, so there's no school to worry about," she said on Ashleigh's behalf. "As long as she stays in the tack room, where it's warm, I don't see any harm. Jonas is right here, and Dreamer *does* seem to respond better to Ashleigh than to anyone else."

Mr. Griffen nodded his approval. "Just make sure

you stay in the tack room so you don't end up with pneumonia," he cautioned.

Ashleigh nodded and headed for the house. When she entered the kitchen, she noticed there was a note stuck to the refrigerator door saying that Mona had called. *Only two more spaces left for race camp,* the note said. Ashleigh crumpled the note and tossed it into the garbage can. Even if money were to fall out of the sky at that moment, she wouldn't be able to leave Dreamer to go to race camp.

The next twenty-four hours passed in a haze as Ashleigh spent every waking moment tending to the injured mare. Dreamer barely moved, and she showed no interest in her hay or grain. "You've got to eat something, or you won't have the energy to heal yourself," Ashleigh said to the filly as she rubbed a handful of sweet-smelling grass hay enticingly under Dreamer's nose. The gray just wiggled her lips against the hay, knocking it to the straw bedding on the floor.

By late afternoon on the day following Dreamer's accident, Ashleigh was resting in the corner of the stall, feeling as miserable as Dreamer looked, when there was a change in the filly. Ashleigh's head popped up when she heard the straw rustle. Dreamer planted her good leg out in front beside the injured one and grunted mightily as she attempted to heave herself to her feet.

Ashleigh wasn't sure what to do. She couldn't help the filly without getting in the way and risking injury herself. The only thing she could think to do was to speak calmly and keep the gray from panicking. On the third try, Dreamer heaved herself to her feet and stood swaying on unsteady legs. Ashleigh tiptoed to the stall door and motioned for Jonas to get her parents.

"Good girl," she crooned as Dreamer shuffled forward on three legs and dipped her nose deeply into her water bucket. "Are you hungry, sweetie?" Ashleigh asked as she held out a handful of hay. She smiled when the Thoroughbred lipped the hay from her palm and munched slowly, but Dreamer refused more hay after the second handful. By the time Ashleigh's parents arrived, the filly was standing quietly in the center of her stall with her head hung in misery.

"Can we give her something to stop the pain?" Ashleigh asked.

Mrs. Griffen entered the stall with a grain bucket, but Dreamer refused to even smell the feed. "Dr. Frankel doesn't want to deaden all the pain," she said. "If Dreamer thinks there's nothing wrong with her leg, she'll put weight on it and undo everything the doctors have worked on."

Mr. Griffen nodded toward the house. "Why don't you go grab a bite to eat? We've got chores to do, and Dr. Frankel will be here soon."

Ashleigh grabbed a peanut butter sandwich, eating it on the way back to the barn. She thought about everything Dreamer had been through since the race, and her sandwich began to lose its flavor. Soon she couldn't force herself to take another bite. She heard a familiar nicker and looked up to see Stardust with her neck stretched over the fence, begging for attention. She went to the mare, leaning her cheek against Stardust's fuzzy winter coat. "I'm sorry I haven't been paying any attention to you, but Dreamer needs me now. You understand, don't you?" She rubbed the long white blaze on the mare's head. What would she do if anything ever happened to Stardust? Ashleigh shuddered. She couldn't even bear to think of it.

Stardust bobbed her head and stretched her lips toward Ashleigh's sandwich. Ashleigh smiled briefly and offered it to the chestnut. "I wasn't going to finish it anyway." She kissed the mare on the nose and continued to the barn.

Everyone was busy doing the evening chores when she entered the barn. She peeked in on Dreamer. The filly stood in the center of her stall. Her head hung low, and she grunted in pain as she shifted unsteadily on her three good legs. Ashleigh thought of all the pain the filly had endured, and wondered if they were doing the right thing. What if Dreamer suffered through all of the treatment but the leg didn't mend and she had to be put down anyway?

She thought of Mr. Rosen waving his handful of winning tickets on race day and scowled. He hadn't even called to see if Dreamer had made it. How could anyone be so uncaring?

Ashleigh picked up a pitchfork and went to the first stall.

The barn phone rang, and Caroline jumped up to get it. Ashleigh saw the disappointed look on her face when she found out the call wasn't one of her friends.

"It's Mona," Caroline said. "She wants to know if you can go for a ride."

Ashleigh forked a load of dirty straw into the wheelbarrow. "I'd better not," she said. "Dreamer needs to be taken care of, and it's getting pretty late." She caught the concerned glance her parents exchanged, and wondered why they should worry about her staying home and doing her chores.

Mr. Griffen handed Ashleigh a hay net to hang. "Are you sure you don't want to take a quick ride?" he asked.

"The weather is supposed to turn bad soon. This might be one of the last chances you get for a while."

Caroline put Mona on hold for a moment. "I'll finish your chores for you, Ash," she volunteered. "You've been stuck in this barn ever since you got back from the track yesterday. You should take a break and get out for a while. Stardust misses you."

Ashleigh frowned as she stared at her family. Why did they care whether or not she went for a ride? She didn't *feel* like riding at the moment. And what if Stardust slipped on a patch of ice and ended up just like Dreamer?

"Caroline's right, dear," Mrs. Griffen said. "I think a ride would do you good."

Ashleigh pursed her lips and sighed. She could see that her family wanted her to go. "Tell Mona I'll meet her in twenty minutes," she said. Whether she wanted to or not, she was going for a ride. She grabbed her riding boots and went to saddle Stardust.

Mona was just trotting down the driveway when Ashleigh led her mare from the barn. She mounted up and turned her collar against the chill, then reluctantly joined her friend on the trail.

"How's Dreamer doing?" Mona asked.

Ashleigh shook her head. "Not very good. She's in a lot of pain, and at this point I'm not really sure if she's going to make it." She rocked with the rhythm of Stardust's gait, thinking about the way the big gray had been before the accident. "You know, I used to beg my parents to let us keep one of the foals so we could race it ourselves, but now I'm not sure that's such a good idea."

Mona's head snapped up. "What do you mean? You're always talking about owning racehorses."

Ashleigh shrugged. "I know." She shifted uneasily in the saddle. "I'm just not sure about a few things right now." She looked straight ahead, trying to think of something to say to change the subject. "Where are we going today?"

Mona stared at her curiously for a moment before she answered. "We could ride to the forest trails," she suggested. "I heard some of the breeding farms along the way had new foals this weekend. We might be able to see them from the trail."

"I don't want to be gone for very long," Ashleigh said. "This is the first time I've been away from Dreamer since the accident. I don't want to be out on the trail if she needs me."

"Then we'll ride fast," Mona said, and asked Frisky to pick up the pace.

They trotted and cantered down the dirt path. When they came to the first farm, they were disappointed to find that the broodmares had all been put in the barn for the night. The next farm still had its mares in the pasture, but there were no foals. They continued on, hoping that the farm ahead would have some new foals.

"What's that?" Ashleigh pointed to the edge of the tree line.

"Where?" Mona stood in the stirrups to see.

Ashleigh moved Stardust forward. "Right over there," she said. "It looks like a horse."

Mona squinted into the distance. "It *is* a horse! And there's more of them!"

As they rode closer, Ashleigh could count at least six mares and two young foals running loose in the field at the edge of the forest. She could also make out the figure of a person standing in the shadows. "I bet that's the farmer. Let's go see if he needs help getting his mares back into the field."

They asked the horses for a trot, posting in time to the two-beat gait. When they drew near, the person in the shadows turned in surprise and then bolted into the forest.

"What's the matter with him?" Mona asked as they heard the sound of footfalls moving frantically into the deep woods.

"It's Vince!" Ashleigh cried in surprise. "What would he be doing . . ." But she didn't need to finish the question. The answer lay right in front of her. Vince had struck again, and this time the victims were a number of expensive broodmares.

"He cut the wires." Mona pointed to the break in the fence where each strand of fencing had been snipped with wire cutters.

Ashleigh swung down from Stardust and tied her to the nearest tree. "That bay mare is caught in the fence," she said. "Mona, you run and find the owner. I'll hold the mare and keep her from fighting the wire."

Ashleigh quieted the broodmare and slowly reached down to free the leg that was caught in the wire. "Easy," she soothed as she tried to untangle the wire. At the sound of the metal fence moving, the bay snorted and tried to get away. "Whoa, whoa!" Ashleigh cried. "You're making things worse!" She calmed the mare again and decided to wait for help. She knew she couldn't do this by herself. The sight of the gaping cut on the mare's leg made her feel queasy inside.

After a few minutes Mona returned with the owner of the horses, an armload of halters, and a can of sweet feed. "This is Mr. Turner," she said, introducing a tall man with broad shoulders.

With the man's help, they quickly untangled the bay mare and rounded up the rest of the broodmares.

"You should tell Mr. Turner what you saw," Mona said.

Ashleigh's eyes cut to where the owner stood, staring

expectantly. "I'm not sure it was him," she whispered to her friend, shooting Mona a look to silence her.

"Tell him!" Mona demanded. "You *know* it was him. You saw his face!"

"Do you know who did this?" Mr. Turner asked as he folded his arms over his broad chest and waited for an answer.

Ashleigh turned to face the man. She shoved her hands deep into the pockets of her jeans and took a deep breath. "I've got no way to prove it, but I think it was Vince Tully. I saw him standing at the edge of the woods, and he ran off when we came up."

"I know that boy," Mr. Turner said. "He's no good. If he's cutting through the woods, I'll have somebody waiting for him when he comes out the other side." He tipped his hat to the girls. "Thanks for your help."

Ashleigh went to Stardust and mounted up. Secretly she hoped they would catch Vince, but when the big bully found out that she had told on him, he was really going to be angry with her. Who knew what he'd do? She watched Mr. Turner lead the limping mare back to his barn. She closed her eyes, still seeing the awful cut the mare had received from the wire. She sighed in defeat. She was tired of all the damage that had been done to perfectly good horses because of careless people. "I've got to get home," she said to Mona as she turned Stardust and started back down the trail.

They rode in silence the entire way home. When they reached the spot where they usually parted, Mona stopped her.

"Do you want to go for a ride tomorrow after school, Ash?" Mona asked. "We could ride over to the Wortons' and see what's happening with the race camp."

Ashleigh shook her head and bumped Stardust into a canter without looking back at her friend. She knew if she turned around, she'd see the same worried look on Mona's face that her parents had worn just an hour before. Why couldn't they all stop worrying about her? She was fine. Dreamer was the one they needed to worry about. It was her life that would never be the same again.

She cantered the rest of the way to Edgardale without glancing back at her best friend or toward the Wortons' farm and their race camp. She wasn't interesting in going to the camp anymore; she wasn't interested in riding at all.

Ashleigh rose early the next morning and went to visit Dreamer before school. Her parents had insisted that she sleep in her own bed the night before, so she was anxious to see how the filly had fared without her during the long, cold night. Dreamer was in the same condition as Ashleigh had left her the night before—pained and depressed.

Ashleigh entered the stall and spent some time massaging the filly's neck and speaking encouraging words to her. After a few minutes Dreamer seemed to perk up, and she hobbled to her hay net for her breakfast. "Good girl," Ashleigh said, feeling a small spark of hope.

She hated to leave for school, but she had no choice. The bus was due in ten minutes. "Don't worry, Dreamer. My parents and Jonas will take good care of you while I'm at school," she said, giving the filly one last affectionate pat. She paid a quick visit to Stardust, then zipped her coat against the cold and made her way to the bus stop. She was surprised to see that Mona wasn't there. She looked down the road, hoping to see her friend trotting toward the bus, but Mona was nowhere in sight. Ashleigh boarded the bus and prepared to spend a long day at school.

School was a never-ending series of gathering homework assignments and staring out windows, wondering how Dreamer was doing. At least she didn't have to worry about Vince, she thought. He was missing from school that day. She felt her stomach knot. Had Mr. Turner caught the bully? Was Vince being punished because she had told on him, and would he place the blame on her? Her shoulders slumped. It was just one more thing to add to her list of troubles.

At lunchtime Ashleigh was surprised to see Mona, Jamie, and Lynne sitting in the hall in front of the cafeteria, seated behind a big table of baked goods. "You didn't tell me you were doing a bake sale," she said in confusion, feeling left out. "Why didn't you ask me to help?"

Mona, Jamie, and Lynne all looked to each other for the answer.

"Um . . . we knew you've been feeling kind of down

lately," Jamie said as she made change for a half-dozen cookies for one of their schoolmates. "So we didn't want to bother you."

Ashleigh wasn't sure why, but the sight of all three of her friends sitting there without her made her even lonelier inside. She rearranged the books in her arms and sighed. *Today is going to be just as bad as the past couple of days,* she thought.

Mona handed her a big sugar cookie. "Are you sure you don't want to go for a ride after school?"

Ashleigh bit into the cookie, wondering who would pay a quarter for something that tasted so bland. She shrugged. "No, I'd better not go today. I've got a lot of things to do." She noticed the way Mona's eyes shifted toward the other two girls in silent communication, and felt more left out than ever. The cookie formed a lump in her throat, and she had trouble swallowing. "I'll see you later," she said, and walked away.

That afternoon when she got home from school, Ashleigh noticed several cars parked in the driveway. She recognized the Gardners' car, and the white sports car parked next to it looked like the one Jamie's parents drove.

"Are we having company tonight?" Ashleigh asked when she entered the hallway. She could hear excited chatter coming from the living room.

"Yes," Mr. Griffen replied. "Actually, *you* are." He saw the doubtful look in Ashleigh's eyes and wagged a finger at her. "Your mother and I are tired of seeing you moping around here, Ash. It's not going to change anything with Dreamer's condition. All it does is make you and everyone else miserable. So your friends have a special surprise for you."

Ashleigh had no idea what was going on. It wasn't her birthday. That was still several months away. Why would everyone gather at her house—especially when there was nothing to celebrate?

Mrs. Griffen waved Ashleigh into the living room. "Since this was your idea, Mona, I think you should be the one to tell Ashleigh about the surprise."

"Well," Mona began as she turned to her best friend, "you've been really sad lately, and I know it's because of Dreamer. But it kind of seems like you've given up on your dream of working with racehorses and becoming a jockey."

Ashleigh felt her stomach tighten. Her friend was right. In the last few days she *had* become disenchanted with racing.

Mona continued. "I know how badly you wanted to go to the Wortons' race camp when you first found out about it, but lately you've been so caught up with taking care of Dreamer after her accident . . . well, I thought that maybe if you could go to camp and work with racehorses again, you might get your dream back." She paused, making sure she had Ashleigh's full attention. "Ash, you're going to camp!"

Everyone in the room exploded in a round of applause. Ashleigh just stood there, knowing that they expected her to be excited about going to camp, but she couldn't work up the enthusiasm. She looked at the people standing around her. "But we don't have the money," she said.

Mrs. Griffen hugged Ashleigh to her. "Everyone pitched in," she said. "Mona gave the money she had saved for her saddle. Rory emptied his piggy bank. Caroline donated her baby-sitting money, and Jamie and Lynne had the bake sale at school. Your father and Jonas and I also pitched in." She smiled at Ashleigh. "With the help of your friends and family, you're going to that camp!"

Ashleigh felt as though she were on a stage with the spotlight pointed at her. All of her friends and family were waiting for a response. Rory stared up at her with a toothy grin, so proud that he had contributed. Jamie and Lynne smiled and gave her a thumbs-up. And Mona . . . Ashleigh knew how much that new saddle meant to her friend. Yet she had sacrificed it in order to send Ashleigh to race camp.

In the suspended moment of time between her mother's words and the answer that Ashleigh was expected to give, she felt ashamed. She really didn't want to go to the race camp anymore, but how could she refuse when everyone had worked so hard to make sure she could go? The weight of their stares grew until she knew she had to respond. She forced a smile to her face. "Thanks, everyone," she managed to say. "This really means a lot to me."

It really does, Ashleigh thought. Not the camp, but the fact that they cared so much for her. Ashleigh decided then and there that even if she didn't want to go to camp anymore, she'd go and act as though she enjoyed every minute of it.

"I'll call the Wortons to reserve your spot as soon as everyone leaves," Mrs. Griffen said.

Ashleigh went down to the barn with her friends to visit with the horses. Stardust was happy to have all the attention.

"I've been neglecting you a lot lately," Ashleigh said as she fed the mare a carrot. "But I guess you'll have to get used to me not being around as much, since I'll be going to the race camp now." She smiled at her friends, trying to remain cheerful.

Everyone grew quiet when they came to Dreamer's stall. The big mare was standing in the middle of her stall with her injured leg cocked out in front of her to take the pressure off.

Jamie leaned over the stall door. "Wow, it's hard to believe she was racing only a few days ago."

"I know," Ashleigh sighed sadly. "I keep thinking how different it might have been if Mr. Rosen had listened to Mike and scratched her from that race."

Jonas stepped out of the tack room and joined them. "Hello, ladies." He turned to Ashleigh. "I forgot to tell you—Mike stopped by today to check on Dreamer. He said to give you his regards." He looked in at the filly and scratched his head. "It seems to me that this little girl is looking a mite perkier today."

Ashleigh studied Dreamer, thinking that Jonas might be right. It wasn't a big change, but the filly definitely seemed better.

Mrs. Gardner poked her head into the barn. "Time to go, Mona. Dinner is waiting."

"We've got to go, too," Lynne said. "Congratulations, Ash. We're really happy we could help you make it to camp."

Ashleigh hugged each of her friends and Jonas, too. The old groom's cheeks grew pink, but he looked very pleased. "You guys are the best!" Ashleigh said. She walked her friends to their cars, then went to the house for dinner.

When she entered the kitchen, she immediately knew that something was wrong. Her entire family stood around the table with long, worried faces. "What happened?" Ashleigh asked in alarm. "Is everything all right?"

Mrs. Griffen pursed her lips. "Ash," she began, then paused. "I can't believe this has happened after all the trouble everyone went to. But I just called the Wortons, and Mrs. Worton told me the race camp is full. We couldn't get you in."

Ashleigh took off her jacket and folded it over her arm. She wasn't sure if she should feel disappointed or relieved. But her friends and family had gone through so much trouble to send her to the camp.

Mr. Griffen took Ashleigh's jacket from her and hung it on a peg in the hallway. "Let's sit down to dinner. We can figure out what we're going to do later."

The meal was a quiet affair. Ashleigh felt bad for her family. They had really wanted her to go to camp. Maybe she would ride over to the Wortons' farm the next day and beg them to let her in. Then again, she really wanted to spend more time with Dreamer. She didn't need to go to camp.

She finished dinner and did her homework, then went to the barn to check on the horses one last time.

She gave Stardust a carrot and then went to

Dreamer's stall, hoping the filly might feel well enough for a treat. "Hey, girl," she said as she entered the stall. She reached out to run her hand over the gray's neck. She paused at the base of Dreamer's ears, feeling the unusual hotness there. "Jonas," she called loudly, "come quick. I think Dreamer has a fever."

Ashleigh ran to the house to get her parents while Jonas called the vet from the barn phone.

Dr. Frankel arrived twenty minutes later. He examined the mare, shaking his head as he went. Finally he put away his equipment and came back to talk to the Griffens.

"We're going to have to watch this filly around the clock for the next couple of days," he said. "I'm going to give her another shot to help reduce the swelling in the leg, and I'll leave a supply of antibiotics that you'll need to administer every eight hours. She could be picking up an infection in that leg. If that happens, we're in a lot of trouble."

Ashleigh felt so helpless. "What did I do wrong?" she asked Dr. Frankel. "I stayed with her and kept her calm, and we've been giving her all of her medication. . . ." Her voice trailed off as a large lump settled in her throat.

Dr. Frankel put a comforting hand on her shoulder. "You've done a good job, Ashleigh," he assured her. "Sometimes these things happen. I wouldn't worry.

The antibiotic and the other drugs should take care of the problem. We haven't lost this filly yet." He administered several shots and left a set of written instructions along with a bunch of pills.

Ashleigh stayed after everyone else had gone up to the house. Dreamer stood with her muzzle just inches off the floor, her ears flopped in defeat. "Poor baby," Ashleigh crooned, running her hand lightly down the gray's neck. "This never should have happened to you. You should be worrying about when your next bucket of oats is coming, not about fighting a fever or mending a leg."

Dreamer shifted her weight and grunted in pain. Ashleigh wished there was something she could do for the filly, but Dr. Frankel had done everything he could. All they could do now was wait and see if time and nature would heal Dreamer's leg. *At least I don't have to go to the race camp,* Ashleigh thought. Now she could devote all of her time to helping Dreamer get well.

7

Ashleigh hopped off the school bus and ran down the driveway. She hated having to go to school when one of the horses needed her. Jonas and her parents were excellent with the horses, but Ashleigh couldn't help feeling that nothing was the same without her there.

"How is she?" Ashleigh asked Jonas as she dropped her schoolbooks onto the desk in the office and followed him to Dreamer's stall.

"We've been keeping a pretty close eye on her all day," the stable hand said. "I think she's on the mend, but we're not out of the woods yet. Her temperature is still running at a hundred and two degrees. It has to come down a little."

Ashleigh let herself into the stall. "It's a good thing I'm not going to race camp," she said. "Now I'll be here to take care of you." She heard a lonesome nicker from the next stall and felt a stab of guilt. She patted Dreamer and whispered in her ear, "I'll be back later. I've got to go visit with Stardust for a while."

She went to the tack room to grab a handful of carrots and the bucket brush before she visited her mare. "Hey, girl," she said as she entered the stall and handed the mare a carrot. She noted the tangles in Stardust's mane and frowned. She really had been neglecting her own horse. She pulled out the currycomb and started on the chestnut's woolly coat.

The telephone rang in the distance, and she heard Caroline holler from the far stall, "Somebody else might as well get that. It's never for me anymore."

Mr. Griffen grinned at his older daughter and answered the phone. He spoke for several minutes, and then hung up the phone and called for Ashleigh and the rest of the family.

Ashleigh looked out of the stall. "Was that Mona?"

Mr. Griffen shook his head. "No, it was the Wortons." He motioned for Ashleigh to join him by the office. He smiled broadly. "It looks like you'll be going to camp after all, Ash."

"What?" Ashleigh was astonished. "How?" She tried not to sound too disappointed, but this was the worst possible time for her to be away from the farm. Dreamer and Stardust needed her!

Mr. Griffen gave them the details of the phone conversation. "Seems that a cousin of Mr. Worton has a son who got into a bit of trouble. In order to keep him out of juvenile hall, he has to complete a program, and part of it involves working with animals. He'll need a partner for the camp."

Ashleigh looked perplexed. "That's odd. Why would he have to work with animals?"

Caroline loaded the dishes into the dishwasher. "There was a kid at our school who got into trouble for being mean to his neighbor's dog. They made him work with the animals at the animal shelter so he would learn respect for them."

Ashleigh shook her head. "It seems to me that if he was mean to animals, I wouldn't want him near another one."

Mrs. Griffen looked concerned. "Will Ashleigh be safe working with this boy? What kind of trouble was he in?"

"The Wortons assured me that the boy is harmless. He's more of a prankster with a lot of energy," Mr. Griffen said. "And they'll be well supervised. They offered us the spot at half the cost. Ashleigh can start camp with all the other kids this coming Saturday."

Ashleigh's mind churned. She didn't want to go to camp now, but she knew everyone had worked so hard to send her. She couldn't refuse without seeming like a spoiled brat. And if she could go to the camp at half the cost, they would be able to give Mona back the money she had saved for her saddle. She suggested it to her parents.

Mrs. Griffen looked at her daughter with pride in her eyes. "I think that's a wonderful idea, Ash." She beamed. "See, everything worked out for the best!"

Ash went back to Stardust's stall and hugged her horse's neck tightly. She wasn't so sure her mother was right, but she hoped so.

For the rest of the week Ashleigh spent all of her after-school time with Dreamer and Stardust. Dreamer's temperature had finally come down to normal. That made Ashleigh feel a little better about being gone for race camp for several days out of the week.

Vince had been absent from school for days, making Ashleigh's life a whole lot easier. She could move freely around the school without worrying about being the object of the bully's taunts.

When Saturday morning arrived, Ashleigh rolled out of bed and pulled on her jeans and a sweatshirt. Only a month before, this camp had been so important to her. And now, though she should have been thrilled to go, she wasn't looking forward to it. What if she did something wrong, and the horse she was looking after ended up hurt?

After a bowl of hot oatmeal, toast, and juice, her mother drove her to the Wortons'. "Do you want me to go in with you for a little bit?" Mrs. Griffen asked.

Ashleigh took a deep breath and glanced toward the barn. All the kids were arriving, and their happy chatter filled the air. She waved to a girl and boy she recognized from school. "No, I'll be okay, Mom. I'll see you later."

As she walked to the large white training barn, she wondered which one of the kids would be her partner. She inspected each of the boys, trying to determine if any of them looked like a troublemaker. They all appeared normal to her.

Ashleigh felt a small tingle of excitement as she entered the barn and saw all the beautiful Thoroughbreds with their heads leaning over their stall doors, their new leather halters with brass nameplates hanging on a peg nearby. Small evergreen trees in planters decorated the aisle, and matching blankets in the Wortons' colors were folded over the blanket bar near the spacious tack room.

She tamped down the feeling of excitement. She

was there because her family and friends wanted her there. She wasn't going to get attached to her assigned horse. She glanced at the beautiful Thoroughbreds, whose coats were sleek despite the chill of winter. Which one would she be assigned to? She noticed that one of the horses was the same color as Dream Time.

Mr. and Mrs. Worton entered the barn with clipboards in their hands. "All right, kids, listen up," Mr. Worton called over the roar of excited voices. "My name is Dan Worton, and this is my wife, Jane. We're putting on this workshop, and we'll spend the first hour matching you up with your partner and your racehorse, and giving you the rules you'll need to follow for the race camp."

Mrs. Worton brushed her short dark hair behind her ears and consulted her clipboard. She smiled at everyone as she spoke. "I'm going to match you with your partner now. When I call your name, please step forward," she instructed. "Once you have your campmate, I want you to stand with that person and wait for your assigned horse."

Ashleigh eyed the crowd of kids. In a few minutes she'd have her campmate. She hoped her partner wasn't too terrible, but what exactly could she expect from someone in trouble with the law? She eyed the boys again. They all seemed nice enough. She waited while

Mrs. Worton called out the names. After everyone was partnered, Ashleigh stood alone in the middle of the aisle.

Mrs. Worton glanced over the edge of her clipboard. "Oh, Ashleigh, your partner's parents called. They said that Vince was going to be an hour late. He should be here soon."

"Vince?" Ashleigh felt her stomach flop. It couldn't be. There were plenty of other kids named Vince. She couldn't possibly be so unlucky.

Mrs. Worton nodded. "Vince Tully is his name. I believe he goes to your school. Do you know him?"

Ashleigh sat down hard on a bale of straw and took a deep breath. She was already doubtful about being here. How could she possibly stay at camp with Vince as her partner?

Molly and Gus, the two kids from Ashleigh's school, looked at her with sympathy. Ashleigh blew out her breath in a defeated sigh.

Mrs. Worton took a seat beside Ashleigh on the bale. "Is there a problem, Ashleigh?" she asked in concern. "I explained to your parents that this boy had been in a bit of trouble with the law. We didn't feel he'd be a problem with other kids," she said. "You'll be well supervised, but if you're having second thoughts about this, we'd be happy to refund your money." She smiled encouragingly. "I'm sure we can find someone to take your place if you'd rather go home."

Ashleigh thought about all the shining faces of her friends and family as they told her about the sacrifices they had made so she could go to race camp. She bit her bottom lip, trying to decide what to do. If she quit, she'd be letting everyone down. She decided she couldn't do that to them. She would finish the camp. But she promised herself she wouldn't get attached to her racehorse, and she wouldn't let Vince get the best of her. "It's okay," she said to Mrs. Worton. "I'm going to finish camp."

"Attagirl!" Mrs. Worton said as she patted Ashleigh on the back, then jumped to her feet. "It's time to assign the horses." She motioned for everyone to come close, then she turned back to Ashleigh. "Your assigned horse will be here about the time Vince arrives. We weren't expecting the extra two campers, so we've had to bring in an extra horse for the program."

Ashleigh watched as each set of kids was assigned a beautiful Thoroughbred to work with. She was surprised to learn that all of the horses were maidens, meaning they had never won a race on an official racetrack. The horses had already been in training for ninety days before they came to the camp and would be ready to run their first race at the end of the camp.

It would be the job of each pair of students to work with the Wortons, and with the special guests that would be brought in, to establish a feeding program and training schedule that would best benefit their horse. Jockeys would be brought in from the local racetracks to exercise the horses on the Wortons' training track. The race camp would culminate in a final weekend in which each horse would be entered in a real race.

Ashleigh felt the old tingle of excitement bubble up, but it was hampered by the new dread that came from knowing what dangers awaited a horse in training. Still, she wondered what her assigned horse would look like. Would it be tall and elegant like Molly's bay horse, or midsized and heavily muscled like Gus's chestnut?

The Wortons continued with the program. The next item on the agenda was the tack box. Mrs. Worton passed out a list of everything that was supposed to be in the tack box and made it very clear that each camper would be responsible for the tack and grooming tools inside. Lost items would have to be replaced at the camper's expense. Ashleigh made doubly sure all of their items were there. She knew her parents couldn't afford to replace the big items like the exercise saddle or race bridle.

As she was finishing her checklist, she heard the sound of a car door slamming. A moment later she heard Vince's loud voice as he spoke with the Wortons. She knew the time had come for her to face her worst enemy. Ashleigh counted each footfall as the tall, dark-haired boy clomped down the aisle. When he stopped beside her, she stood from her kneeling position in front of the shiny silver tack box and turned to face her new partner.

"Hello, Vince," she said in the coldest tone she could muster. She saw the shock that first registered on his face, then the pure delight in his brown eyes when he realized who she was.

Ashleigh took a deep breath and bit her bottom lip. She had never been a quitter. But at this moment she had never wanted to quit anything more in her life.

8

"Smashleigh!" Vince crowed, and then winced when Mr. Worton placed a firm hand on his shoulder and squeezed.

"You're here for a purpose, young man," Mr. Worton warned. "You'll behave while you're at camp, and follow our rules. If I find any infractions, you'll be expelled. And I know it's of the utmost importance that you complete this program," he added in a tone that insinuated he knew all the details of Vince's punishment.

"Yes, sir," Vince said in the respectful voice he used to deceive his teachers at school.

Mr. Worton let go of Vince's shoulder. "I'll be watching you," he said in an authoritative voice, letting Vince know that he wasn't fooled.

Mrs. Worton was instructing the campers on the

use of pitchforks and manure rakes when a small, white two-horse trailer pulled up outside the barn. "Ashleigh, Vince," she said, "your horse is here. His name is Broadway Raider."

Ashleigh walked quickly to the front of the barn, curious to see what their horse looked like. Vince dragged his feet, stubbornly refusing to show enthusiasm for anything. The camp kids nearest the door craned their necks to get a peek at the new horse. A young groom who introduced himself as Robert Walker jumped from the truck to let the horse out.

After a loud clattering of hooves on the trailer floorboards, the horse emerged from the trailer. Ashleigh hesitated for a second, waiting to see if another horse would be unloaded. The little seal-brown colt with the shaggy coat that stood before her couldn't possibly be theirs! His coat was long and dirty, and he was short and muscular, more like a quarter horse than the tall, lanky Thoroughbreds she was used to. He didn't look anything like the rest of the horses at the camp.

"I'll take him to his stall for you," Robert volunteered. "After that, he's all yours."

Vince was waiting at the barn door. He walked beside Ashleigh as they followed the new horse back to his stall. The bully seemed oblivious to the fact that their horse was not half as nice as the other campers' horses, but he did notice that the others were snickering as they walked by.

"What's their problem?" Vince mumbled under his breath.

"Don't let Raider's looks fool you," Robert told them. "This colt has some run in him. He just needs to grow up a bit and figure it out for himself."

When they reached the stall, Vince was called away to catch up on the details he'd missed. Ashleigh spent the time getting acquainted with Raider. The stocky brown colt walked around his stall with his head lowered, sniffing the bedding and inspecting his feed buckets. When he was finished with his inspection he came to the front of the stall and stuck his head over the door.

"Hi there," Ashleigh said as she gave Raider a scratch behind the ears. "You're a friendly fellow." The words had no more than left her mouth when Raider flipped his muzzle and nipped her on the arm. Ashleigh jumped back. "Ouch!" she cried in dismay. "What did he do that for?"

Raider bobbed his head and blew through his lips.

Robert laughed as he removed the colt's halter and hung it on the peg outside the door. "That means he likes you," he said.

Ashleigh looked at him suspiciously. She rubbed the

spot on her arm where Raider had bitten her. "He has an awful funny way of showing it," she grouched. "I think you're teasing me."

Robert leaned on the door and patted the horse. "No, really. If somebody comes up to the stall that Raider doesn't like, he'll go to the back of the stall. There are not too many people he takes a fancy to. I'd say you're probably one of the lucky few." Ashleigh wasn't sure if the word *lucky* was what she'd had in mind.

Mr. Worton walked over to inspect the new horse, and Ashleigh waited to see what would happen. Just as the groom had predicted, when the farm owner approached, the brown colt walked to the back of the stall and stood along the back wall. Several of the camp kids came over to have a look, and Raider remained in the back of his stall.

"That's odd," Ashleigh commented.

Robert shrugged. "He's just picky about who he chooses to give his attention to."

At that moment Vince returned with his list of instructions. "They take this stuff way too seriously," he grumbled.

Ashleigh was surprised to see Raider walk to the front of the stall when he heard Vince's voice. He poked his head over the door and sniffed the boy.

"I guess he's not *too* picky," Ashleigh said to Robert with a laugh.

Vince eyeballed her, knowing that he was somehow the object of an inside joke, but not sure how to take it. Instead he turned his attention back to the brown colt, laughing when Raider nuzzled his face with his bewhiskered muzzle.

"Hey, look, he likes me," Vince said as he reached out to stroke the colt's neck.

Quick as a cat, Raider twisted his lips and nipped Vince on the soft underside of the arm. The boy yelped in pain but quickly retaliated, reaching out and pinching the Thoroughbred right on the soft curve of his nostril. Raider snorted and backed up several steps, then came forward curiously and stuck his muzzle into Vince's sweatshirt.

Robert tipped his hat and laughed. "Well, I guess you two have an understanding. I'll leave you all to get better acquainted." He winked at Ashleigh and left.

Vince sat on the tack box outside of Raider's stall and sulked. "Stupid horse," he said as he rubbed his arm.

Ashleigh wasn't quite sure what to do. She had a sulky boy and a four-legged clown to deal with—and thirty whole days to put up with them both.

"I thought he liked me," Vince said as he moved away to avoid Raider's questing lips as the horse reached over the stall door.

Ashleigh thought about keeping silent, but like it or not, she was stuck with Vince and Raider for the next month. She decided to tell Vince what Robert had told her. "He does like you," she said reluctantly.

"Yeah, right," Vince scoffed. "If he did, he wouldn't have bitten me."

Once again Ashleigh thought about keeping silent. She didn't need to pass on the information Raider's groom had given her. But she reconsidered as she watched Vince sit there with a hurt look on his face when moments before he had seemed to take great delight in thinking that he had made a connection with the animal. Vince had been put into this program to help him learn respect for animals. She didn't owe Vince anything, but if it would help future victims of the bully's mean pranks, then she owed it to the animals to try to help.

Ashleigh walked over to the tack box and sat down beside Vince. "He really does like you," she insisted. "His groom, Robert, told me that if Raider doesn't like someone, he won't even come to the front of the stall. If he likes you, he'll stand with his head over the door and bite."

Vince curled his lips in disdain. "Like I'm going to believe a stupid story like that."

Ashleigh knew the bully would only believe what he saw with his own eyes. She signaled to the boy from school. "Hey, Gus, can you come here a minute?"

Gus put down the brushes he was setting in order

and strolled over to Raider's stall. Ashleigh kept the boy there for several minutes, talking about the camp so Vince could notice Raider's reaction. As she had predicted, Raider walked to the back of his stall during the discussion.

Vince stood when Gus left. "Here, boy." He smooched to Raider, as though he were calling a dog.

The brown colt's ears flicked in confusion.

"Don't smooch to him," Ashleigh said. "In horse talk, a smooch means 'giddyap.' Just call him over by his name."

Vince spoke Raider's name and extended his hand over the door. Raider bobbed his head and walked to the front of his stall. They each patted the brown colt and fussed over him for several minutes. Ashleigh noted his bewhiskered chin and the long hair growing out of his ears. They'd have to trim that long hair if he was to begin looking like the other horses in the barn.

Raider wiggled his lips to nip again, but this time Ashleigh knew the signs and was able to avoid the pinch. Vince wasn't quite so lucky. He sucked in his breath and gritted his teeth at the pain, then once again pinched Raider on the end of the nose, smiling when the racehorse blew through his lips and returned for more affection.

Ashleigh smiled. Vince didn't know it yet, but he was on his way to becoming a horse fan. She just wished Vince were more friendly so he'd be easier to work with.

"Okay, kids," Mrs. Worton said as she clapped her hands to get everyone's attention. "We're going to take a quick lunch break. We'll be serving cheeseburgers up at the house. I'll expect everyone back at the barn by one o'clock."

Ashleigh stopped Mrs. Worton as the rest of the kids filed out. She noticed Vince had hung back to listen to her conversation. She ignored him and spoke to Mrs. Worton. "We've got a horse that's been pretty sick. I'd like to go home and see how she's doing while the rest of the kids are at lunch."

Mrs. Worton nodded in understanding. "Yes, your parents were telling me about that poor filly. You go ahead and go home. I'll see you back here in an hour."

Ashleigh went to get her gloves from the top of the tack box. Vince sneered at her as she walked to the door.

"Hey, Smashleigh," the bully hollered after her. "Why don't you do me a favor and forget about coming back?"

Vince's cackling laugh followed her out the door. Ashleigh jammed her hands into her pockets and hunched her shoulders against the cold breeze. At the moment, it sounded like an excellent suggestion.

Ashleigh checked on the filly, who was lying in her stall, stretched out on her side. She didn't want to startle Dreamer, which might make the horse try to scramble to get up, so she didn't open the door. Instead, she leaned her chin on the top of the door and frowned. It worried her when Dreamer got up or down. It was the most dangerous time for her bad leg.

She studied the filly, wondering how long it would be before Dreamer would be out of danger. The veterinarian had warned them that legs took a long time to heal, but it already seemed as though it had been forever since Dreamer's fateful race. How long before they could quit worrying about her and know that she was going to be okay?

She turned and walked toward the house, kicking off her boots on the front porch before entering. She glanced at the clock in the hallway. She was due back at race camp in forty-five minutes. Her stomach growled, and she went to the cupboard to get the jar of peanut butter and two slices of bread.

She poured herself a glass of milk and sat down at the table. Scenes from the morning's race camp ran through her mind. Of all the people in the world that she could have had for a partner, why did it have to be Vince? She thought about the mean taunt he had hurled at her as she walked from the barn that morning. Maybe she should do as he suggested and stay home. Camp wasn't going to be any fun, anyway—especially with Vince as a partner. And Dreamer needed her at Edgardale.

Ashleigh bit into her sandwich with resolve. There was no reason for her to go back to camp. She swung her feet happily under the chair and smiled. Vince could finish race camp by himself. She was going to stay home and take care of Dreamer!

Caroline entered the kitchen and stopped in her tracks when she saw Ashleigh sitting at the table. "What are you doing here?" she said in confusion. "You're supposed to be at camp."

Ashleigh's legs stopped their motion, and she rested her feet on the rung of the chair. "I'm not going back to camp," she said as she stared at her sister defiantly.

Caroline arched a perfectly plucked eyebrow. "What do you mean, you're not going back to camp?"

Ashleigh shrugged. "It won't do me any good, and I've got Vince Tully as my partner. And besides, Dreamer needs me here." She looked away from Caroline's burning stare and turned her attention back to her meal.

"How do you figure camp won't do you any good?" Caroline cried. "All you've talked about your whole life is racing horses and being a jockey. They're bringing in all those great trainers and jockeys. There will be all kinds of great things you can learn, Ash."

Ashleigh glared at her sister. "Maybe I don't want to race horses anymore," she snapped defensively. "Maybe I don't want to have another horse get hurt like Dreamer." She tossed her sandwich back on the plate and shoved it away from her.

Caroline huffed in exasperation. "You can't give up on your dream just because one stupid horse got hurt."

Ashleigh stood up so quickly, the table slid across the floor a few inches. "Dreamer is not a stupid horse!" Her hands balled at her sides, and she felt her face begin to grow hot. Her sister didn't know what she was talking about.

"Maybe Dreamer's not a stupid horse," Caroline

countered, "but I've certainly got to wonder about you."

Ashleigh took a step forward. She was so angry, she was shaking, and she could feel the tears gathering in her eyes. "What do you mean by that?" she said.

"I mean exactly what I said!" Caroline cried. "You've got a family and friends who care enough about you that they spent their savings to send you to that stupid race camp in hopes that you would rediscover your dream and get back to being your old self. But you let one horse's accident get to you, and you give up on everything! You've never been a quitter, Ash," Caroline said with a sad note in her voice. "Don't start now." She turned and walked from the room.

"I'm not a quitter!" Ashleigh hollered after her, but her sister's words cut to the bone. She stood in the middle of the kitchen with her hands on her hips and felt the tears sliding down her cheeks. She wanted to shout something terrible and mean at her sister for making her feel this way, but she knew that what Caroline said was true. She *had* given up on her dream.

She jammed her hands into her pockets and hung her head, trying to remember what it felt like when she had been so sure about racing. She scrunched her lips. Maybe race camp would help her find that old feeling again. She thought about Dreamer and sighed. She didn't know if she'd ever feel that way again, but Caroline was right—she owed it to her friends and family to at least try.

She glanced at the clock. She had ten minutes to make it back to the Wortons'. She grabbed her coat, pulled on her boots, and ran the whole way back to race camp.

She made it to the barn just as everyone was filing back from lunch.

"Oh, great," Vince said as he scowled at Ashleigh. "You decided to come back."

Ashleigh shot him a withering stare. "You're not getting rid of me that easily, Vince Bully." She smiled sweetly at his shocked expression. "Oh, I mean Tully."

Mrs. Worton entered the barn aisle and clapped her hands. "Listen up, everyone." She waited until she had each kid's attention before continuing on. "We're going to start this afternoon off by bringing each horse out of its stall, one at a time, and introducing the horse and its pedigree to everyone." She scanned the crowd of camp attendees. "I know most of you have grown up around horses, but for those who are just getting started, Mr. Worton is going to give you a demonstration of how we halter and lead a Thoroughbred, plus hooking a horse into the crossties and grooming."

A low grumble stirred through the crowd of kids, most of whom had experience with horses.

Mr. Worton smiled. "Come now, everyone has to start somewhere. Not all of you are at the same level. For those of you who are lucky enough to have horses of your own, just think of this as a refresher course, and a chance to help out someone who is just getting started."

Vince looked at Ashleigh and snickered. "Yeah, like I need your help with anything."

Ashleigh narrowed her eyes. She knew Vince had never worked with horses before—except to let them out of their field. If he wanted to be a smarty-pants, she'd give him just enough rope to tangle himself up.

They watched the haltering demonstration Mr. Worton gave. Ashleigh actually picked up a new trick for walking a rowdy horse. When Mr. Worton handled an excited Thoroughbred that liked to lean on him and walk all over his shoes, the farm owner put his right arm up parallel to the ground and held it stiff so his elbow was pointed into the horse's neck. Each time the prancing horse leaned into him, the elbow helped keep the proper distance between horse and human; also, the pointed elbow soon became uncomfortable for the horse and would discourage it from leaning on the handler.

"All right, kids," Mrs. Worton said as she raised a handful of pedigree papers. "Let's go to work. I want each Thoroughbred haltered, and when I call your name, I would like one teammate to walk the horse up the aisle and stand with the horse while we read the pedigree, and the next teammate to take the animal back to its stall."

Vince huffed. "That's easy enough. This camp is supposed to be punishment. This is a walk in the park."

Ashleigh wanted to wipe the bratty smile off the bully's face. She hoped he wasn't going to be this much of a pain the entire month. She suspected part of his bravado might come from trying to cover up that he really didn't know anything about horses. She decided to test her theory. "Here, Vince," she said as she handed him the leather halter. "You put the halter on Raider and take him down the aisle first."

"Me?" Vince squeaked. "Why me? You're the horse expert. Why don't you do it?" he challenged.

Ashleigh said nothing; she just stepped back with a challenging smile.

"Nothing to it," he bragged as he held up the halter, trying to decide which part went over the nose.

Ashleigh left him to halter the biting colt while she rearranged the grooming tools in the tack box. She laughed to herself when she heard Vince cry out in pain, knowing that Raider had nipped him again. A moment later there was a rustling sound coming from the stall, and Vince swore under his breath, begging Raider to get off his foot.

Mr. Worton came over to see how they were doing. He quickly sized up the situation and exchanged a conspiratorial wink with Ashleigh as he motioned to her to come peek into the stall.

It took every ounce of strength Ashleigh had to keep from laughing when confronted with the sight of Raider and Vince. The brown colt stood in the middle of the stall with a piece of Vince's shirt hanging from his lips. The halter was on his head, but Vince had put it on upside down, so the long piece that ran on the underside of the halter now ran down the middle of Raider's face, with the buckle latched under the colt's throat instead of up by his ear.

Vince stood holding the lead shank, which was attached to the ring that dangled between the colt's nostrils. He looked so proud of himself that Ashleigh didn't have the heart to laugh at him.

Mr. Worton stepped into the stall. "Let me just make a few minor adjustments," he said with a slight smile as he repositioned the halter. "Ashleigh, Vince will lead the colt out to show him, but you can stand nearby in case he needs help."

Ashleigh nodded and opened the door, waiting for everyone to pass out of the stall. On the way out the door, Raider swished his long dark tail, catching her square in the face. She sucked in her breath at the sudden sting and blinked her watering eyes. Then she sighed. With a colt like Raider, she wouldn't have to worry about getting emotionally attached. He was almost as big a bully as Vince.

As they took the colt down the aisle, Ashleigh could hear the quiet laughter of the other kids. She understood why they were making fun of Raider—he looked like a horse that had just been brought out of a winter pasture. But Vince, who didn't know anything about horses, couldn't understand why everyone was making fun of his horse. In fact, he thought they were laughing at him, and it made him angry.

"Just ignore them," Ashleigh said when they returned Raider to his stall. She explained why the other kids had been laughing, and went on, "We'll get him brushed up and pull his mane to shorten it, and he'll look just as good as the other horses do." She knew that was a big stretch on the truth—Raider would probably never look as good as the other elegant Thoroughbreds—but it seemed to make Vince happy.

They spent the rest of the afternoon learning about

tack and setting up feeding programs for the horses. At the end of the day, Mr. Worton announced that the next morning they would be joined by two-time Derby-winning trainer Ronnie Egbert.

Ashleigh felt a small jolt of excitement. It was hard to think about getting involved with another racehorse when she pictured Dreamer lying injured in her stall, but the mention of the Derby winner sparked some of those old feelings again.

That night when she got home, she made a quick stop by Dreamer's stall, promising to come right back as soon as she was finished with Stardust. Her pretty chestnut mare munched on the carrot Ashleigh offered and cocked her hip in contentment while Ashleigh groomed every inch of her body. As she worked, Ashleigh told the mare all about Vince and the difficulty she was having with him.

Mrs. Griffen came over and stood at the door to Stardust's stall. "I'm sorry to be eavesdropping, Ash, but did I hear you say Vince is your partner?" she asked in an alarmed tone. "Are you going to be all right?"

Ashleigh nodded. "He was okay today. He doesn't know anything about horses, and he made a lot of mistakes that made him seem more silly than bullyish." She tossed the last brush into the bucket and patted Stardust. "Now it's Dreamer's turn."

Mrs. Griffen opened the door to the gray's stall. "Dr. Frankel was here today," she said as she let Ashleigh into the stall. "He says Dreamer has made a big improvement in the last couple of days. Next week he's going to change her cast to something that will allow her to move a little more."

Ashleigh was shocked. That was great news, but she hadn't been there to share the special moment with Dreamer—she had been at camp, putting up with Vince's wisecracks. She gave the filly a big hug, feeling that she had somehow been lax in her duties. Dreamer grunted as she shifted in the stall. Ashleigh's lips drew taut in concern. The big filly was improving, but she was still a long way from being completely out of danger.

Mr. Griffen grabbed the empty hay net from the stall. "I'll get her some grass hay, Ash. Why don't you open the top door at the back of her stall and let her look out and get some fresh air for a little while?"

Dreamer slowly swung her body around at the sound of the opening door. She hobbled over on three legs and stood looking out at the colts and fillies frolicking in the pasture. Ashleigh put a hand on the filly's neck, feeling the tremble of muscle as she watched the young horses run across the field.

Ashleigh frowned in confusion. Dreamer acted as

though she wanted to join the yearlings in their private race. Why would the filly ever want to race again when she'd been hurt so badly on the track? It didn't make sense. Ashleigh thought about how excited she used to get when her parents took her to the races. She frowned. Except for that small spark of interest she'd felt when Mrs. Worton had mentioned the trainer who'd won the Kentucky Derby twice, she still felt dead inside about racing.

Dreamer bobbed her head and flared her nostrils as she watched the colts and fillies frolicking in the pasture. Ashleigh closed the door before the filly got too excited and did something to hurt herself. She set down the grooming box and brushed the gray, speaking calming words to settle her down. When Dreamer seemed more at ease, she let herself out of the stall. She leaned on the stall door, glancing at the injured Thoroughbred. Dreamer was improving, but she still wasn't out of the danger zone yet. Would the filly heal enough to be able to withstand the extra weight a broodmare would carry?

And what about me? Ashleigh wondered. Would racing ever be a thrill for her again, or would she always see Dreamer's breakdown and hear her groans of pain as she came out of the anesthetic and fought for her life? How could race camp help her get over that? She jammed her hands into her coat pockets and walked toward the house. In front of her was another day of putting up with Vince and Raider and worrying about Dreamer. At that moment she almost wished she had stuck to her plan and not returned to race camp.

Vince beat Ashleigh to the barn for their second day of race camp. Everyone was busy learning how to saddle and bridle their racehorses while they waited for the star trainer and the gallop boys and girls to arrive at the farm. Mr. Worton had suggested that Ashleigh be the one to saddle and bridle the colt that morning. She could barely resist sticking her tongue out at Vince when he asked Mr. Worton why she got to saddle first and the farm owner told the boy that Ashleigh was more experienced and could teach him how it was properly done.

She fumbled with the girth buckles, trying to pull the girth a little tighter, but Raider had learned the age-old trick of horses everywhere and had sucked in a big breath, expanding his rib cage so the saddle would fit more loosely when he let out his breath. Raider pinned his ears with the next pull, and Ashleigh dodged a cow kick. She smacked the naughty colt in the belly with the flat of her hand, causing him to jump forward onto Vince's foot.

"Hey, watch what you're doing!" Vince grouched as he pulled the toe of his boot out from under Raider's hoof.

Ashleigh hid a grin. She was feeling better already. She took the lead from Vince and tied Raider to the ring on the wall of his stall while they waited for the celebrated trainer to arrive.

Soon Mr. Egbert was there and everyone gathered around the famous trainer. Ashleigh found herself crowding in with the rest of the kids, asking questions about his two Derby wins and the great horses he had trained. Even though she wasn't enthusiastic about sending Raider into a race, she couldn't resist the chance to stand next to the famous trainer and listen to the answers he gave to the cascade of questions.

"All right, everyone," Mr. Worton called. "Let's give Mr. Egbert some room to breathe. Our exercise people are here. We're going to take our horses out four at a time for a slow gallop. Mr. Egbert will give us a lecture and help us set up a training schedule for each horse afterward."

Ashleigh and Vince went back to Raider's stall to wait their turn. Several of the boys from nearby stalls were making bets on whose horse would be the best at the end of camp. Raider chose that moment to stick his head over the stall door.

Tommy, a lanky kid with dark hair, said, "Guess you two are out of the running," and laughed.

Vince stepped forward and put on his best scowl. "Oh, yeah? How much you want to bet?"

Ashleigh tugged at his sleeve. "Don't make that bet, Vince," she whispered. "Tommy has one of the best-pedigreed horses here, and he knows it."

Vince jerked his elbow away, continuing to stare down the other kid. "I'll take that fancy watch you're wearing if you feel like parting with it," Vince said, full of bravado.

Tommy was about to accept the bet when his partner elbowed him in the ribs. "You can't make bets like that, Tommy. If your mom and dad found out, you'd be in a lot of trouble."

"All right," Vince said. "I've got it!" He smiled at his own cleverness. "Whoever loses has to clean the other person's tack and stalls on the last day of camp, and they've got to wear a shirt that says Loser in big letters on the front and back." He cackled with glee and turned back to Ashleigh. "What?" he said when he noted the doubtful look on her face.

Ashleigh pursed her lips and shook her head. "You shouldn't have made that bet," she said. "There's no way Raider will beat Flying Troubadour."

Vince's eyes narrowed. "He will so, and you're going to help him do it. You're the big horse expert here. I've heard the kids at school talk about how good you are." He crossed his arms and glared at her. "Besides, you're the reason I'm here in the first place!"

Ashleigh gulped hard. Vince knew that she had told on him.

The bully took a menacing step forward. "The way I see it, you owe me, girl. And you're going to repay me by helping Raider win his first race."

Ashleigh turned and walked away. She wasn't going to do any such thing. She didn't owe Vince anything, and there was no way Raider could possibly beat the competition.

Everyone went to the training track to watch the horses gallop. Mr. Egbert made comments on how each horse was galloping, what its attitude was, and how it traveled. He pointed out how Molly's horse was lugging in toward the rail, indicating that she might be having some pain in her legs, or perhaps that the bit was causing her discomfort. Another team's horse was refusing to switch leads on the turn, which would cause him to run out, or move toward the outside rail, during a race and cost him many lengths.

Ashleigh found the trainer's observations very interesting. The man didn't miss much. He saw things that nobody else had picked up on. She found herself wondering what he would say about Raider. The horse didn't look as though he could run, but maybe he'd surprise them.

A sharp jab to the ribs brought Ashleigh out of her wonderings. She turned to glare at Vince.

"What do you think he's going to say about our horse?" Vince said excitedly.

Ashleigh was surprised by the enthusiasm she saw on the bully's face. Most likely it was because of the bet and had nothing to do with the horse, but at least he was getting involved. She shrugged. "His groom seemed to think hee immature. We'll have to wait and see how he goes."

Raider's group was next to go. Vince insisted that he had paid close attention to the bridling session, and he wanted to put the bridle on Raider. Ashleigh handed him the leather gallop bridle with the rubber-clad reins and went to check the saddle. Just as she suspected, Raider had relaxed and the saddle was now loose. She quickly pulled the girth strap snug. Raider swished his tail and stomped his foot in displeasure.

"There," Vince said, and stood back proudly.

Ashleigh couldn't hold back her grin. The chin strap was in Raider's mouth along with the bit, and the brow band was back behind the brown colt's ears.

Vince fisted his hands on his hips and glared menacingly. "What are you laughing about? The bridle is on fine."

Ashleigh continued to grin. "It was a good effort for

your first time, Vince, but let me show you where you went wrong. Raider won't travel right like this." She pulled the brow band back into place and fished the chin strap out of the horse's mouth. "There, now it's perfect!"

Vince beamed, and Ashleigh was relieved that it hadn't turned into a fight. She winced when she felt a slug in the shoulder.

"You know, Smashleigh, you're all right for a girl," the bully said with a smile. "Let's go out there and beat those other three horses in our group."

Ashleigh snapped a lead rope onto Raider's bit and handed the rope to Vince. "We're only galloping this morning," she said. "We don't have a speed work until next week. Mr. Egbert just wants to see how all the horses are going so we can make out a training chart to get us up to our first race."

"Oh," Vince said in disappointment as he walked Raider out of the barn. "Well, maybe we'll outgallop them. I want to show that stupid Tommy that our horse is the best."

They heard the snickers and snide remarks as soon as Raider came out of the barn.

"All right, kids," Mrs. Worton scolded. "Let's not make fun of each other's horses. We all know Raider wasn't supposed to be part of this program. He's a little behind the rest of the horses, so we don't expect him to be at the same level."

Vince frowned and mumbled under his breath. Ashleigh helped him hold the colt still so Mr. Egbert could leg the rider up into the saddle. Raider immediately began to dance sideways. Ashleigh took over the lead rope and gave a warning jerk on the bit.

The exercise rider put his feet in the irons and grinned. "I see you've done this before," he said as he knotted his reins. "I'm in good hands."

Ashleigh smiled her thanks. She led Raider out to the track where the other three horses waited and turned him loose, then joined Vince and Mr. Egbert on the rail to watch the one-mile gallop. Since the track was only six furlongs long, the riders had to backtrack the horses around to the bottom turn to get in a mile.

Raider tossed his head and skittered sideways, bumping into the horse nearest him. When the other horse pinned his ears, Raider kicked out, barely missing the other animal. Mr. Egbert made some notes on his pad, and Vince craned his neck, trying to read the notes.

The riders turned the horses in the correct direction and asked them for a trot, then broke into a slow canter. Raider immediately dropped his head and started to buck. The exercise rider popped him with his crop and got his head up, but Raider continued with the game, galloping several lengths in good form, then tugging at the bit to see if he could catch his rider off guard to buck again.

Ashleigh pursed her lips and tried to ignore the sound of laughter and the mean jabs at Raider. The colt would never make it to the race. If he continued like this, they'd be lucky to get him to gallop in a straight line.

Mr. Egbert gave them an understanding nod. "Looks like you two have some work to do."

Ashleigh jammed her hands into the pockets of her jeans and sighed. It would take a miracle to get Raider ready in time for his first race.

Several days later Ashleigh was sitting in the school cafeteria with her friends when Vince plopped his lunch tray down beside her. She hadn't told any of her friends that the boy was her camp partner because she wanted them to think she was enjoying the race camp. She couldn't resist smiling when she saw the way Mona's and Jamie's eyes bugged out of their heads at the sight of Vince sitting at their table. They were even more shocked when he began talking horses instead of teasing her.

"We've got to figure a way to make this horse pay attention and run," Vince said between bites of his pizza. "I know he can beat those other horses. I just know it!"

Vince didn't seem to notice that Ashleigh's friends were looking at him as though he had two heads. He kept rambling on about race camp. When he was finished, he picked up his tray and left, calling back over his shoulder. "It's Wednesday—we've got camp after school. You'd better figure out something that will help our horse."

She had a lot of explaining to do to her friends after Vince left. "I'm sorry I didn't mention it before," Ashleigh said. "But I was afraid you guys would worry about me."

Mona stared after Vince's departing form. "He's changed since I last saw him," she said. "There weren't any mean words coming out of his mouth. He actually seems human now . . . well, almost."

They laughed as they put away their lunches and went to their classes.

It wasn't long before the school day was over and Ashleigh was making a last-minute check on Dreamer and Stardust before she went to camp. This was the day their assigned jockeys would arrive. They would breeze the horses for three-eighths of a mile. *All of them except for Raider,* Ashleigh reminded herself. Raider would continue with long, slow gallops until he was behaving properly.

Mrs. Griffen poked her head into Stardust's stall. "You've got company."

Ashleigh glanced up expecting to see Mona. She was shocked to see Vince standing in the barn aisle. "What's up?" she asked, wondering what would bring Vince to her barn when he knew he would see her in another half hour.

Vince leaned his tall, thin frame against the barn wall and fumbled nervously with the halter hanging on the peg. "Look, Ashleigh. I know you're not really into this camp . . . which kind of surprises me because you're such a racehorse nut." He colored slightly, sensing that he had hit a nerve. "But I've never gotten to do anything like this before, and . . ." He paused, evidently not sure how to explain himself. He took a deep breath and rambled on. "This is important to me. I want to see Raider do good, but I don't know how to help him. And you don't seem to want to help. Is it because you're still mad at me for all the mean stuff I did to you? Are you trying to sabotage Raider because of me?"

Ashleigh shook her head and let herself out of Stardust's stall. She led Vince over to where Dreamer stood with her head hanging over the back door of the stall, watching the activities outside.

"Wow!" Vince said when he saw the cast on the filly's leg. "What happened to her?"

Ashleigh explained the entire story, including the fact that there was still a chance the leg wouldn't heal and Dreamer would have to be destroyed. "I just don't know if I can stand to watch another horse race again," she admitted.

Vince looked at her doubtfully. "But how can you give up on all horses just because one got hurt? That's stupid, Smashleigh!"

Ashleigh's head snapped up. She was flabbergasted. Here she was sharing her private feelings with this bully and he was calling her names. "You don't understand!" Ashleigh cried, and turned away.

"Sure I do," Vince shot back defensively. "You got hurt, and now you're too afraid to try again. I'd call that just plain chicken."

Ashleigh doubled her fists at her sides and stood there with her mouth open, waiting for the words she wanted to hurl at Vince, but nothing would come.

In the heavy silence that hung between them, Ashleigh heard the faint but distinct clang of a starting gate popping open at the farm next door. A second later, a clatter of hooves and a snort came from

Dreamer's stall as the filly hobbled in circles around the confined area. Ashleigh dashed into the stall. "Whoa, Dreamer!" she cried.

Dreamer continued to dodge around the stall on three legs, snorting and cocking her tail over her back.

"Run and get my parents!" Ashleigh cried as she tried to stop Dreamer from moving around too much. She knew that if the mare lost her balance and had to use her casted leg for support, she would shatter the leg.

Mr. and Mrs. Griffen came running. They entered the stall and helped her hold the horse still.

Ashleigh felt the tears streaming down her face. "Is she hurt? Did she reinjure the leg?"

Mr. Griffen knelt in the straw to examine Dreamer's leg. "I think it's okay, but we'll call the vet just to be sure."

Ashleigh saw the strange look Vince was giving her. She wiped angrily at the tears on her cheeks, but at this point she didn't really care what he thought. All she cared about was Dreamer being okay. "Why does she do that?" she asked in confusion. "Why does Dreamer still try to run even if it means she'll hurt herself again?"

Mrs. Griffen pulled Ashleigh into her embrace. "It's what she's born to do, Ash," she said as she handed her daughter a tissue. "Thoroughbreds are born to run. It's in their blood. Dreamer doesn't understand that she might be injured. She just knows that she wants to run with the other horses."

Mr. Griffen stood and dusted his hands on his pants. "Look, Ash, your mother and I both know that you've been reluctant to have anything to do with racing since Dreamer's accident. But don't let one lousy owner cause you to lose sight of your dreams. You've got to understand that accidents can happen anywhere, anytime. Keeping a horse locked up for its own protection doesn't work. They're meant to run. You've got to let them do what they're born to do."

Vince spoke up. "The kids at school say that you want to be a jockey someday. Are you going to give up on that before you even get a chance to find out if you're any good at it?" He laughed his bully's laugh. "Seems to me that horse knows more about what she wants than you do."

Ashleigh wanted to slap the smirk right off Vince's face, but deep down she knew he was right. Still, she couldn't help feeling apprehensive when she thought about watching another horse race.

"Come on," Mrs. Griffen said. "You two are going to be late for camp. I'll drive you over."

Ashleigh didn't feel like going to camp, but her spirits improved when they arrived and she discovered that Jack Dale was among the attending jockeys. He recognized her and came over to speak to her when he saw her at Raider's stall. They chatted for a while, and she filled him in on Dreamer's condition. Then he turned his attention to Raider.

"What have you got here?" he said, peering in at the horse.

Raider lifted his head from the straw he had been picking through and came to the front to hang his head over the door.

Vince perked up. "See, he likes this guy." He turned to the jockey. "You've got to be our jockey. Raider doesn't like just anybody. He'll go good for you."

Ashleigh frowned. "Mr. Dale probably isn't interested in riding our horse, Vince. There are a lot of good horses here for him to choose from."

"You can call me Jack," the jockey said as he dodged a nip from Raider. "And I'll ride this horse as a special favor to you," he told Ashleigh. "Let me go tell the Wortons I'll be your rider."

Ashleigh could hardly believe her ears. Jack Dale was going to ride their horse as a favor to her!

Vince slapped her a high five and smiled. "This is it, Smashleigh. This is the break we've been waiting for. I don't want to wear that Loser T-shirt, so don't blow it!"

Ashleigh ignored Vince's taunts. She felt a small tingle of excitement work its way back into her heart. She thought of Dreamer racing around her stall despite the pain. And if Dreamer could still try, she could, too. Maybe her dream of racing wasn't lost to her forever.

Ashleigh and Vince stood on the rail as Jack back-tracked Raider around the bottom turn, getting him prepared for a lone gallop, since the colt wasn't ready to breeze with the other horses yet.

Raider tossed his head and trotted sideways down the track, but the experienced jockey bowed the colt's neck and lined him out. Raider seemed to know that he'd met his match. When they turned the right way around the track, the colt tucked his chin toward his chest and broke into a canter.

The three horses that Raider was supposed to breeze with stepped onto the track for a half-mile work.

"I wish Raider was working with those horses," Vince said. "He could beat them all."

As Raider galloped past Ashleigh and Vince, Jack smiled at them over his shoulder. Ashleigh looked up the track to where the three horses were just turning around and breaking into an easy gallop. "Raider is going so slow, these horses will catch him at the top of the stretch," she calculated, frowning worriedly.

"So?" Vince shrugged. "They're working faster, so they'll be on the inside rail and Raider will be on the outside."

"But will Jack be able to control him when three horses go racing past?" Ashleigh raised her brows. "You know how Raider likes to buck."

"Hey, Vince," Tommy yelled down the rail. "When's your horse going to get out of the baby class and run with the real horses?"

Ashleigh laid a steadying hand on Vince's arm while the rest of the kids laughed. They followed Raider's progress as the three working horses gained on him. Raider was just at the top of the homestretch when the breezing horses caught up to him. Jack stood in the irons as the brown colt tossed his head in the air and zigzagged for several yards before taking the bit in his teeth and charging ahead.

"Come on, Raider, go!" Vince said.

Ashleigh shot him a quieting look. "He's supposed to be just galloping, like Mr. Egbert suggested," she reminded him. "We don't want Raider to work yet." She watched Jack pull with all his might, leaning back and putting all his weight into the bit. Raider held steady, galloping down the stretch behind the horses, but Ashleigh could see that he wanted to catch them. Maybe there was hope for the colt after all.

Jack returned with the horse, hopping out of the saddle as soon as he left the track. He patted Raider's neck. "I know there're not very many people here who have any confidence in this colt, but I think you might have yourselves a sleeper."

"Do you really think so?" Ashleigh asked in surprise.

Jack loosened the girth and ran the stirrups up the leathers. "He's got a lot of power. He just needs to stay focused. I'll be back to gallop him on Saturday. I'll see you then."

Ashleigh spent the next several days going to school and coming home to tend to Dreamer and Stardust. She found herself mentioning Raider and his wild antics when she groomed the two mares. Surprisingly enough, she was actually looking forward to the next day of camp.

When Saturday finally arrived, Ashleigh walked into the Wortons' barn to discover everyone in a state of confusion. "What's the matter?" she asked Vince.

The big kid shrugged and tried to look nonchalant. "A lot of people are missing their grooming kits."

Ashleigh ran to their tack box. "Is ours here?"

Vince smiled confidently. "Of course it is. And so are Molly's and Gus's and anyone's who didn't make fun of Raider."

Ashleigh stifled a laugh. "You didn't!"

Vince winked. "Of course not. They'll find them when they go to get their grain ration."

Ashleigh smiled. At least Vince was finally limiting his pranks to those who deserved it. She grabbed the tack and went to saddle Raider. Mr. Egbert had scheduled Raider to gallop with the rest of his group today, and Ashleigh found herself hoping that he would do well.

Jack showed up fifteen minutes later, and they walked Raider out with the other three horses.

"He's looking better," Ashleigh said as the jockeys backtracked the four horses. "He's finally starting to lose that shaggy winter coat and look like a real racehorse," she observed. "Let's hope he acts like one today."

As the horses turned down the racetrack, Jack tucked Raider in behind the first two colts and let another horse pass him on the outside. Raider tossed his head and cantered sideways, bumping into the rear ends of the horses ahead of him. One of the colts kicked out, and that was all the reason Raider needed to start bucking again.

"Oh, no." Ashleigh groaned. "What'll we do now?"

Mr. Egbert stepped up to the fence rail. "Maybe we've got the training chart wrong on this colt. I think Raider needs a lot of strong gallops to keep his mind occupied." He scribbled some notes in his pad and tucked it into his jacket pocket. "I'll see that Mr. Worton gets somebody to gallop this colt every day while you guys are in school. On Wednesday we'll be busting them out of the starting gate."

Ashleigh and Vince finished the day in disappointment. Their horse didn't seem to be showing any improvement. And to make matters worse, when everyone showed up for camp the next morning, Tommy brought a bright pink T-shirt with Loser in big letters on the front and the back.

"I got it in size large just for you," Tommy said to Vince with a laugh.

"Good," Vince sneered. "Because it will look like a dress when you're wearing it!"

Jack showed up for the morning gallop. "What's all the fuss about?" he asked.

Ashleigh explained the Loser T-shirt to him, and the jockey had a good laugh.

"We'll get this colt straightened out," he said with a wink as he followed Raider outside and accepted a leg up. He checked his saddle and knotted his reins, then leaned down to pat the colt on the neck. "You're going to gallop like a gentleman today, son." He gave them a smile and joined the other three horses on the track.

This time, when they turned and broke into a canter, Raider leaned into the bit and got a jump on the other horses, galloping a length ahead of the rest. Jack held him in that position as they moved steadily around the track.

"Looks like a different horse altogether this morning," Mr. Egbert observed. "Jack knows horses. He'll bring out the best in this colt."

Ashleigh reserved her judgment until Raider had made it all the way around the track and pulled up. She gave Vince a quiet high five as they went to pick up their horse from the exit gate.

"He did great!" Jack said as he dismounted and loosened the girth. "Wednesday will be our telltale ride. If he breaks out of the gate and works smoothly, I think we've got the problem beaten."

On Wednesday Raider's group of horses was the first scheduled to go to the starting gate. As soon as the Wortons were finished with their instructions,

Ashleigh and Vince ran back to the barn to prepare Raider for the work. Jack was waiting for them when they arrived at the barn. Ashleigh hurriedly gathered the tack, giving Vince the bridle while she saddled the brown colt. Raider tossed his head and stomped his feet, cow-kicking when Ashleigh pulled the girth tight.

"He seems kind of flustered today," Vince said.

Jack laughed and smacked his whip across his shiny black boots. "Of course the colt's nervous. Look at you two." He grinned. "You're running around acting like you're late for the Kentucky Derby. Relax," he advised. "This is just a work out of the gate."

Ashleigh and Vince looked at each other and laughed. They had been so wrapped up in wanting Raider to do well that they had forgotten to do what was best for him.

Ashleigh took a deep breath. "Let's calm down and do this right."

But it was too late. Raider had already picked up on their nervous mood, and Jack couldn't get the colt to settle down on the track. Raider and the rest of the horses had broken from the starting gate several times before coming to race camp, but Raider acted as though he had never seen the big metal contraption before. He was difficult to load and wouldn't stand quietly in the gate.

When they finally popped the latch and the doors banged open, Raider was in the middle of pawing the ground and got a late start. He stood for a second, watching the other three horses run down the track ahead of him, then charged out of the gate and ran about a hundred yards before breaking into a major bucking spree.

Jack managed to stay on and pulled Raider to the outside of the track. "I'll be back in a minute," he called to the gate crew. "You hold that next set of horses for me."

Ashleigh watched as Jack turned Raider down the track and smooched him into a full gallop. The colt bowed his head and worked against the bit, acting like a serious runner. After one lap of the track, the jockey pulled the stubborn colt to a halt and brought him back to the starting gate. "We're going to do it right this time," he said. "Hey, Ronnie," he called to Mr. Egbert. "Can you get behind the gate and give me a push out of here?"

"Sure," Mr. Egbert said. "This colt needs a little extra attention. He's not as far along as the rest of the horses."

Ashleigh was curious. How could Mr. Egbert give the horse a push out of the gate? But as the horses were being loaded, she saw the trainer remove his hat. This time when the gate popped open, Mr. Egbert brought his hat down soundly on Raider's hindquarters, and the brown colt charged out of the starting gate, beating the other horses and gaining lengths as he moved to the rail and ran easily around the top turn.

"Look at him go!" Vince said as he jumped up and down beside Ashleigh.

Ashleigh followed the horses as they came down the homestretch. Tommy's horse made a move to challenge, but Raider pinned his ears and stretched his neck, holding the lead as he crossed the finish line.

"Yes!" Vince crowed, and did a silly victory dance along the rail.

That got him a lecture on poor sportsmanship from Mr. Worton, but it didn't affect Vince's good mood.

They took Raider back to his stall and removed his tack. Ashleigh gathered the wash bucket while Vince led the colt to the wash rack.

"He sure worked nicely that second time around," Jack said.

Vince took the hose and squirted a warm stream of water onto Raider's steaming coat. "How come Raider is so unreliable?" he asked. "One day he works great, and the next day he's a disaster."

Jack shrugged. "He's just very immature."

Ashleigh picked the sponge out of the bucket and

began to scrub the sweat from Raider's coat as she thought about Vince's comment. Her father had always taught her that there were reasons for the ways horses behaved. Why was Raider so inconsistent? She mentally replayed all of his gallops, looking for a pattern. She paused in her scrubbing. "Wait a minute. I think I might have it."

"Have what?" Vince said as he dodged Raider's questing lips.

She turned to Jack. "I think I have the pattern," she said excitedly. "The two times that Raider did well was when he was out in front of the pack. Maybe he's one of those horses that has to be out front, or he quits trying!"

Jack scratched his chin and thought in silence for a moment, then nodded. "You might have something there, Ashleigh. Since all of these horses worked today, we won't start them back galloping until Saturday. We'll try your theory out then." He pointed to Mr. Egbert. "You should go discuss your theory with him and see what he has to say."

Ashleigh gulped. What if she was wrong and she looked like a total fool in front of the big trainer?

"Go on, Ash." Vince gave her a push in Mr. Egbert's direction. "I'll finish Raider's bath."

Ashleigh walked up to the trainer and waited until he noticed her. She had a difficult time getting started, but the trainer smiled and put her at ease, making it a lot easier to say what she had in mind.

"Raider seems to run better when he's out front," she said to the trainer. "The times he's acted really bad were when he was forced to gallop behind the other horses. Maybe he's the kind of horse that has to stay out front." She waited for his reaction, hoping that he wouldn't tell her she was just a dumb kid with a stupid idea.

Mr. Egbert cocked his head and smiled. "You know, I was just on my way to talk to you about that very thing," the trainer said. "You're pretty observant, young lady. You'll make a good trainer someday."

Ashleigh glowed at the praise. "I'd like to be a famous jockey just like Jack someday," she said, feeling the color enter her cheeks.

Mr. Egbert patted her on the back and steered her toward the barn. "I'll keep my eye out for you in a couple of years. I like helping young riders get started."

Ashleigh could hardly wait to get home to tell everyone what the famous trainer had said. It was a memory she would treasure forever!

12

Mona smiled and leaned against the railing beside Ashleigh and Vince as they watched Raider walk off the Wortons' track after his gallop.

"What are you smiling like that for?" Ashleigh said.

Mona grinned. "You're getting back to your old self, Ash. I can tell."

Ashleigh felt a smile creep across her face as she realized her friend was right. She was still apprehensive about racing another horse, but she could also feel a stir of excitement about it. And now Dreamer was doing better, too. Things were definitely looking up!

Jack Dale rode over to where they were standing. "You were right on target, Ashleigh," he said as he dismounted and handed Raider's reins to her.

Ashleigh smiled proudly. Raider had been training

well for the last couple of weeks. Poor Jack had been bucked off a couple of times when they were testing Ashleigh's theory and trying to make Raider run behind the other horses, but the jockey hadn't been hurt—and it had been worth it, because now Raider was training as well as the other horses at camp.

Later that day, Mr. Egbert sat down with all the kids and helped everyone pick a race for their horse. Since none of the horses in the camp were stakes or allowance horses, they would all be placed in a claiming race that fit their class.

Vince looked perplexed. "What's a claiming race?" he asked.

Mr. Worton answered the question. "Each claiming race has a special price tag on it. They can run as low as two thousand dollars at a small track, up to an average of fifty thousand dollars at some of the bigger tracks. The price can go higher, but that's an average," he explained. "Once you enter your horse in that race, any owner or trainer with a current license at that track can put up the money before the race starts, and once the starting gate pops open, that horse belongs to the person who claimed it."

Vince looked shocked. "You mean somebody could buy Raider in his first race?"

There was a round of snickers from the other kids,

and someone whispered, "Who would want him?"

Mr. Worton hushed the noise and continued. "Even if that horse breaks down during that race, he belongs to the person who put up the money to claim him. And if more than one person puts in a claim, they have to shake the peas after the race to see who gets the horse." He saw a few confused looks and explained. "They put a bunch of little balls into a cup, and whoever draws out the one with the black dot gets the horse."

Ashleigh could see that Vince was thinking hard about that bit of information.

Mr. Egbert took over the lecture and explained how the claiming system worked. "The trick," he said, "is to find a race where the claiming price is high enough that nobody will be tempted to claim your horse, but low enough that he can still win. Obviously, if you put a high-money horse in a two-thousand-dollar claiming race, he would probably win the race, but there would be a bunch of people who would put in a claim on him, and you'd lose your expensive horse for a cheap price." He glanced around the room to see if everyone understood the concept. "And it works the same in reverse. If you put a cheap horse in a fifty-thousand-dollar race, he would most likely get beaten by a lot of lengths."

Ashleigh raised her hand to ask a question. "What class of race will most of our horses be in?"

Mr. Egbert smiled appreciatively at the good question. "Most of you will run in a twenty-thousand-dollar class," he said. "A few will run higher, and a couple will run lower. That's what we're going to do today. I'll sit down with each of you and determine what will be the best race for your horse."

Once the lecture ended, everyone went to sit in front of their horse's stall to wait for the trainer. Vince fidgeted as he sat on the bale of straw. Ashleigh noticed him craning his neck to hear what Mr. Egbert had to say to Tommy across the aisle.

"Tommy's horse is going in the twenty-thousand-dollar claimer on Sunday," Vince said. "So that's where we're going, too."

Ashleigh looked doubtful. "That might not be the race Mr. Egbert has picked for Raider. Not all of the horses are running in the same race or even on the same day."

Vince was totally disappointed when Mr. Egbert showed them the race he had picked for Raider. "It's only a ten-thousand-dollar claimer," he said in disgust.

The trainer went over Raider's timed workouts with them. "I really feel that this race is where he belongs," he told Vince.

"But we've got to run against Tommy's horse," the boy protested. "How else will we know which horse is the best?"

Mr. Egbert tipped his hat back on his head and

smiled. "You've got to do what's right for the horse," he said. "Raider will have a lot better chance of winning the smaller claiming race."

Vince pouted as he mulled over that information. "But the actual race won't be any different from the one Tommy's horse is in, right?"

Mr. Egbert showed them the condition book where all the upcoming races were listed. "That's true. It's a six-furlong race, just like Tommy's." He could see where the conversation was going. "It will just be a little more difficult for Raider to win a race like that because the quality of horses will be different."

Vince looked hopeful. "But he could run in it, right?"

Mr. Egbert turned to Ashleigh. "What do you think?"

Ashleigh scanned the pages on the condition book. Here was a decision that could affect Raider's career as a racehorse. She knew Vince wanted to beat Tommy, but she had to make a decision that was best for the horse. "I'm sorry, Vince. I agree with Mr. Egbert."

Vince's eyes grew hard as he crossed his arms and glared at her. Ashleigh knew he would be hard to get along with after she had gone against him, but she had to do what was best for Raider. He wouldn't be hurt any by running in the higher-priced claiming race, but his chances of winning would be a lot weaker.

"All right, then," the trainer said as he stood to leave. "I'll be entering the horses in these races on Wednesday morning. I'll let you know Wednesday night what position we drew for the race."

On Wednesday when they met with Mr. Egbert again, Vince was handed a bit of good news.

"Raider couldn't get into that cheap race," the trainer said. "It was so full, he didn't even make the waiting list. It looks like he'll be in Tommy's race after all."

"Yes!" Vince cried as he punched the air in triumph. "You'd better get that shirt ready," he hollered to Tommy, "because you're going to be wearing it!"

Ashleigh glanced at Mr. Egbert. She could tell by the look on the trainer's face that he was as doubtful about the outcome as she was.

Ashleigh spent the remainder of the week doing her barn chores and fussing over the horses. By Friday the weather had turned a bit warmer. Dreamer was doing so well with her leg that they were able to let her stand out in the small paddock that adjoined her stall. She put Stardust out in the pen next door to keep the gray filly company.

Ashleigh sat on the top rail and smiled as she watched Dreamer move about slowly. It was the filly's courageous effort to walk again that had convinced Ashleigh that she should resume her dream of racing. She stuck a piece of hay between her teeth and chewed on the end. Raider's race was the next day. She faced that thought with excitement and dread. But she knew it was a hurdle she would have to get over in order to get back on track with her racing career.

She hopped down from the fence and walked toward the house. In less than twenty-four hours she'd be back at a real racetrack, helping Vince prepare Raider for the first race of his life. She hoped she could handle the pressure.

Ashleigh rose early on Saturday morning and finished her chores quickly. The final weekend of race camp had arrived. Six horses from the camp would be going to the post that afternoon. It was going to be an eventful day. Not only would she be racing her first horse since Dreamer's breakdown, but the vet was coming before they left for the races to X-ray Dreamer's leg. If the results were good, Dreamer would get an even lighter cast.

She skipped the big breakfast Caroline had made, instead grabbing a Danish and a banana from the counter before going to the barn to do her chores.

"Today's the big day, huh?" Jonas said as he handed her the rations for Stardust and Dreamer.

Ashleigh nodded. "I still think Raider is in over his

head, but Vince has a lot of confidence in him." She patted Stardust and emptied the grain into the chestnut's bucket, then moved on to Dreamer's stall. "I'm hoping for a miracle," she told the old groom. "Vince has actually been pretty nice these last couple of weeks. I'm afraid if his horse loses, he'll revert right back to the same mean-spirited boy he used to be."

"You can always change schools," Jonas teased.

Ashleigh laughed. "I may have to." She grabbed the wheelbarrow and started her morning chores. Dr. Frankel arrived as she was finishing her last stall. He took several different shots of Dreamer's leg. He stood when he finished the last X ray and carefully marked each black plate. "I've got to go to the racetrack today to help in the test barn," he said. "I'll get these developed and bring them with me." He reached over to ruffle Ashleigh's hair. "Don't worry. Everything's going to be fine."

But Ashleigh was worried. She had a horse that was running over his head in the third race that day, and a filly whose future depended on the outcome of the X rays.

She sighed as she went to the house to shower and change for the races. It would do her no good to worry. She shed her horse clothes and turned on the warm shower, letting her troubles wash down the drain.

An hour later her family and Mona crammed into

the old station wagon to make the journey to the racetrack. Ashleigh didn't speak much during the trip. Her mind was too full of worries.

"We're here!" Rory cried when they pulled into the back parking lot at Turfway Park.

Ashleigh felt her stomach twist in knots as she made her way to the gray barn with the green roof, where the Wortons and Mr. Egbert would be waiting for the camp kids. Vince was already there, and he looked in even worse shape than she did. His face was ashen, and he had deep circles under his eyes, as if he had been up half the night.

"We'd better get started," Mr. Worton said. "There're three of you running in the third race, one in the fourth, and two more in the fifth. Let's get busy!"

Ashleigh and Vince brushed Raider until his coat gleamed. "Here," Ashleigh said, handing Vince a small blue flower to braid into Raider's mane.

Vince's brows shot up in surprise. "No way!" he said. "You're not going to make him look like a sissy."

"Oh, come on. Don't be such a wimp," Ashleigh teased. "He's got to have at least one flower for good luck."

Vince looked up at Ashleigh. "Oh, all right. But just one," he said in disgust.

When they were finished, they sat on buckets outside of Raider's stall to wait for the call to the back gate.

When it came, they almost jumped out of their skins.

"This is it," Vince said. "The moment of truth."

Ashleigh noted the worried set of Vince's eyes. For his sake, she hoped Raider ran well. Vince had worked so hard at the camp and made such a change in his personality, he deserved to win this race. Ashleigh extended her hand for Vince to shake. "No matter how we do in this race, I want you to know that I'm really proud to have been your partner. You've done really well with Raider," she said.

Vince blushed at the compliment and went back to fussing with Raider. "He'll win today. You'll see."

Mr. Worton led Raider over for the third race. Ashleigh and Vince were too young to get a trainer's license, so they followed the horse over and waited outside the paddock while Raider was saddled. Mona and the rest of the Griffens were waiting for them by the rail.

When the call for the post parade sounded, Ashleigh dragged Vince over to her favorite spot on the rail. Vince took an entire roll of film while the horses paraded in front of the crowd. Jack smiled at them as he passed, and then stood in the irons while the pony rider bumped the horses into a gallop toward the starting gate, which stood on the other side of the mile track.

Ashleigh held her breath as they loaded the horses

into the gate. She and Vince had worked so hard with Raider. She hoped he would do well.

"I don't think I can stand to watch," Vince said, and covered his eyes. But when the announcer called that all the horses were loaded and ready to run, Vince opened his eyes and craned his neck to see.

"They're off!" the announcer cried.

Ashleigh's breath hitched as she watched Raider break in the air and scramble to catch up.

Tommy elbowed his way in next to them. "Your horse broke lousy," he taunted. "That'll put him back a ways, and we know Raider doesn't like to run in the back of the pack."

"Be quiet, Tommy," Ashleigh snapped. "I don't see your horse in front, either." She kept her eyes glued to the herd of racing Thoroughbreds as they fought for position down the back side. Ashleigh clenched her hands so hard, her fingernails made dents in her palms. She hoped Raider wouldn't be too upset that he was behind other horses and begin to buck. She could see Jack was already struggling with the colt.

"My horse is out front now!" Tommy crowed.

The announcer's voice cut over the roar of the crowd. "Flying Troubadour takes the lead, with Golden Rose running second and Annie's Prince running third."

"Take him to the outside!" Ashleigh cried, wishing Jack could hear her. Maybe if Raider could see daylight in front of him, he would think he was in the lead.

Just as if the horse and rider had heard her call, Raider swung to the outside of the pack and began to gain ground.

Ashleigh bit her lip. "He won't make it if he has to run the whole way on the outside. It's too far," she said to Vince.

They watched as Raider passed several horses on the outside as the field headed into the turn. He was now in fifth place but was forced back onto the rail when several of the lead horses began to fade.

"He's boxed in!" Vince cried. "He's got nowhere to run!"

Ashleigh's parents crowded in behind her. Her father laid a hand on her shoulder. "He's actually sitting in a good spot for the turn," Mr. Griffen said. "He'll save a lot of ground. All he needs is for a hole to open up somewhere."

"Uh-oh, Tommy," one of the boys from camp hollered. "Your horse is starting to fade!"

Tommy jumped up and down, screaming for his horse to continue, but it was obvious the big gray was fading fast.

As the horses came out of the turn, Raider got the

break Ashleigh and Vince were hoping for. The race-camp horse that had had trouble switching leads for the turn switched back into his right lead too soon and drifted off the rail. Jack wasted no time driving Raider up into the hole. When the brown colt saw daylight, he pricked his ears and dug into the track, gaining ground on the leader.

"Go, Raider!" Ashleigh and Vince yelled in unison.

Mona squeezed her arm. "He might do it, Ash! Raider could win this race!"

Ashleigh held her hands in fists, guiding the young colt to his first win, as if she were the one up on his back.

"Broadway Raider moves up to challenge as Flying Troubadour fades and Annie's Prince tries to hang on for the win!" the announcer called.

"Go, Raider!" Ashleigh screamed as the determined colt continued to inch forward, gaining ground with each stride he took. Several lengths before the finish line, Raider poked his nose in front of the first-place horse and pinned his ears as he fought to pass the leader.

"It's Broadway Raider by a head!" the announcer cried over the roar of the crowd.

"We did it!" Vince picked up Ashleigh and swung her in a dizzying circle. "We did it, Smashleigh!"

Mr. Egbert came over to congratulate them on their win. Ashleigh and Vince begged him to pose in the winner's circle with them. As the Wortons and all the camp kids crowded into the photo area, waiting for Jack to bring Raider back to the winner's circle, Ashleigh spotted Dr. Frankel in the crowd. She waved for him and her parents to join them.

Mrs. Griffen gave Ashleigh a big hug. "We've got good news, Ash. Dreamer's X rays came back great! The leg is healing fine, and Dr. Frankel feels that we can breed her next season."

Mr. Griffen gave her a nudge. "Since you were so dedicated to Dreamer during all those difficult days, we're going to let you pick out the stallion," he said. "And who knows? You did so well with Raider that maybe by the time Dreamer's colt arrives, we'll be ready to keep and race one of our own."

Ashleigh's smile was so wide, she thought her face was going to split in two. Jack returned with Raider at that moment, and they moved him into place in the winner's circle.

"Wait!" Vince cried as he pulled something out from under his coat.

Ashleigh laughed with the rest of the camp kids when she saw the pink Loser T-shirt.

"Put it on before we take the win photo," Vince said

with a grin as he tossed the shirt to Tommy. "And make sure you're in plain view in the picture!"

Mr. Worton motioned Ashleigh and Vince forward, handing each of them one of Raider's reins. "You kids deserved this," he said. "I never would have thought this colt could win this race. You guys did great!"

"Ah, gee." Vince blushed as he accepted the compliment. "I would have run out there and carried Raider across the finish line just to see Tommy wearing that pink shirt!"

The camp kids all laughed at the joke. Even Tommy slapped Vince on the back and congratulated him.

As they posed for the win photo, Ashleigh saw Raider's lips twitch, and Vince cried out in pain as the feisty colt nipped him hard on the arm.

Ashleigh laughed and winked at her new friend as the cameras flashed. Thanks to the stubbornness of one bully, the determination of a great filly, and the love of her family and friends, winning races was more than just a dream—it was a reality.

Chris Platt rode her first pony when she was two years old and hasn't been without a horse since. Chris spent five years at racetracks throughout Oregon working as an exercise rider, jockey, and assistant trainer. She currently lives in Reno, Nevada, with her husband, Brad, five horses, three cats, a llama, a potbellied pig, and a parrot. Between writing books, Chris rides endurance horses for a living and drives draft horses for fun in her spare time.